HERBRIELLA GOLD

...In the haunted palace of kutch

[A MAGICAL CLIFF-HANGER]

- By H.V.VORA

Dangerous Serpent

HERBRIELLA GOLD
...In the haunted palace of kutch
[A MAGICAL CLIFF-HANGER]

Originally published in the India

ISBN: 978-81-921311-0-8

Published by RIGI PUBLICATION
777, Street no.9, Krishna Nagar
Khanna-141401 (Punjab) India
Website: www.rigipublication.com
Email: info@rigipublication.com
Phone: +91-9357710014, +91-9465468291

ACKNOWLEDGEMENTS

"My late sister Bhavana Gala's funeral was the cause for me to express my day dreams, weird thoughts and even nightmares on paper. But I wouldn't have dared to take this step, unless J. K. Rowling's 'Harry Potter' has inspired me.

I owe this book to my elder sister Deepa for believing and encouraging me to reach the end. Next thanks goes to Deepali, my niece, very first one to read the manuscript and to give her best suggestions.

My parents though illiterate, have always done their best to get me the best of life. I am grateful to them for buying me story books and all the stuff in my childhood that further helped me to create the sense of writing. I thank all my six sisters, a brother and their family for bearing my tantrums without any word spoken. I thank all my nephews and niece to teach me 'C' for Computer and its usefulness that had enhanced my writing correcting all the grammar mistakes and lot more. For this I thank Microsoft corp. How can I forget to thank my childhood friends Moushami and Nimisha, who influenced the vital character in the story? I would like to thank few publishers who rejected my work to find me the best and right publisher. I must thank my very intelligent publisher Umesh Sehgal who believed in my dreams and shaped them into a book. I am also thankful to Kamal Puri and Amit, the entire staff at RIGI Publication.

One more is left, The One who seeks no thanksgiving as he just wants me to think and dream about him- my imaginary dream man, who is simply with me and will always be.

Last but not the least my sweet little daughter Ammie Vora, whose little wishes always remind me to think big, bigger and the biggest."

Chap-1

THE DOOMSDAY

It was a dark stormy night. Hovering hoots were heard on the top. Freezing winds blew and shrilled about like ghosts. Inside the veil of dark was immense willowy castle sleeping sound. Only the conch shaped window of the cell was still awake. The lobby that ended in the cell seemed dark and gloomy. Few tiny shadows were trying to lurk among the pillars heading towards the cell.

－－－－－

The sight outside the castle was mysterious. The wild roots of dark trees were moving closer to the window. The evil trees spreading their arms and covering the castle looked eager to swallow it. It seemed that they were conspired for something special.

－－－－－

A sudden terrible noise inside the cell was compelling the tiny shadows' to see the matter. The noise got more terrible, as they moved nearer. It was like a banging a metal shield and it stopped at once. All the shadows' tried to peep through the window's crack and could only see the darkness.

－－－－－

By the time, the lingering twigs outside the castle grew in numbers. Under the disguise of the night they were ready to clutch their prey.

－－－－－

Inside the cell, the scene was not so oppressive yet. Various flowers were beautifying on the sidewalls. They were entwined as thickly as the climbers. One by one they were stretching to share out their fragrance with the scope. It looked the entire beauty of nature has been amassed here. But someone's grieve was not allowing herself to feel this beauty. The Queen Olivia-De-Peace, the oldest, the experienced, the only sovereign of this serene colorful world was looking displeased. She was addressing the group of maids who were surrounding someone and one of them holding a lean pitcher. All of them were wearing sap-green robes except the Queen; she was wearing an auburn Queen's gown and crown on her head. One in the hub was in faded brown robe sitting on her knees. She was tied with the ropes. Her hands were joined across with the ropes, which she had tried number of times to get rid of. The maid, who was holding a pitcher, was trying to make her drink from it but she always pushed the pitcher away from her [or the maid herself went aside on purpose]. She was repeatedly pleading the Queen to forgive her. The group of maids loosens the barrier of their hands they had formed around her and waited for the further instructions from the Queen. The Queen too, became considerate, looking towards the woman in the hub she said, "Tulika, you shouldn't be here. This is not the place for you, dear. I ... I can..." and the Queen stopped . . . her nose broaden to smell something . . . it was stinking . . . it was like a rotten egg . . . her wide eyes did not move and she narrowed herself with the fingers blocking her nose. Even the maids moved backward with their fingers on their nose. Moving a little they all stiffen at the place. The flowers on the wall dry out and the cell that was aromatic a moment ago was filled with the awful odor now, it turned murky and...

Suddenly, a callous voice from the side of the gloomy pillar firmly ordered the maid to finish the task immediately. The maid could not disregard the voice. Finally, with the help of others she squeezed the woman's jaw and poured the liquor from the pitcher in her mouth. Although finishing the task successfully the maid herself looked ashamed. Within a moment, the woman threw out the seven mauve threads that expanded into the petals of flower. Eighth time she felt, but nothing came out. The petals lay idle beside when again the voice said,

"DIVULGE" and a greenish smoke flew towards them. As a result, the petals came to life, joined and formed into the human figure instead of the flower.

"TULIKA… You… how is it… I cannot believe…!" said the Queen Olivia astoundingly to the woman who just rose from the petals. She went on changing her sight from the woman who was in the hub to the one who rose from the petals at once. "Then who is she?" the Queen asked without blinking. "And how can one remain hidden under someone else's genre?" The Queen's round innocent face turned red to darkest expressing her soreness.

"Exactly your Highness, this kind is from the earth." The woman with the callous voice provoked the Queen revealing herself out of the gloom. She seemed more than her voice, garbed in bronze robes with black fur around her neck that continued beyond the length of the robes. She had a heart shape face with stout features and a heavy neck. Only her tall stature bears out her dominance. [She was Raflesia- de- rot, the right hand of the Queen, Seldom allowed the queen to take the last decision.]

"Oh! No then who is she, why is she here and how?" the Queen asked pointing towards the woman in the hub to whom she took in as Tulika. And the woman in the hub transformed with the beautiful features and the fairest skin, blue crystal clear eyes but worried now. Even the scope with the people there was charmed with her beauty for a while. However, Raflesia was smart to take the hold back…

"Your Highness" said Raflesia, "She is Romarin. . . who does not belong with us, why she is here that is the point to be considered later, but how. . ." And she grinned viciously towards the woman in the hub, "Well, I can definitely explain you."

"Your Highness, have a mercy on me. I was about to tell you everything…" Tulika – the flower wailed in front of Queen Olivia.

"No, Tulika, you betrayed me." the Queen said with the utmost pain.

"You Kindhearted, give me one chance." Tulika begged her.

"I am helpless." Saying this Queen Olivia turned away from her. Raflesia grabbed the opportunity, she again spelled-with an aim finally and before anyone could make out, the screams of Tulika burned into the fire just broken.

"No… you cannot do this…," said Romarin – the woman in the hub unable to take in Tulika's unexpected end madly moved towards Raflesia, but the maid seized her back so she turned to Queen, "Your Highness, it was not Tulika it was I, I am the culprit. Please Your Highness have a mercy, save her, she is innocent." And she sniveled. She became so desperate that without waiting for the Queen's permission, she instantly bellowed "RAKSHA KAVACHAM" pointing her first finger towards the shrinking flower which now began to turn into ashes. But the white sparkles her spell threw out were diffused by Raflesia. "STOP THIS NONSENSE!" brutal Raflesia snapped Romarin and banged the metal rod she was holding, which was crafted of the several rooty strings bound together under the skull crown and the skull howled at once, flapping out its tongue. "You are not supposed to use the celestial powers," she yelled. [Though being most ignored, Raflesia was chosen so for her unrivaled wit and sense. It seemed that the queen Olivia was under the thumb of her right-hand.]

"No use Romarin, an irreversible spell." She said and blew the smoky ashes of Tulika in air. Wailing Romarin tried hard but could not rescue the ashes of Tulika from vanishing. The cell echoed Raflesia's laugh.

—

Hearing the noise, the tiny shadows tried to see inside the cell but were unable. Then they tried another window. The midnight darkness was helping them to proceed. Finally, the shadow set itself beside the second door followed by the other shadows. As soon as they peeped inside they were jammed. . .

"Who are you?" suddenly Raflesia stopped laughing and talked to the air where the shadows were hiding. This made all of them to lean to see that she has detected. Suddenly she placed her left palm open muttering a bit. The next moment there appeared a bowl filled with water. Raflesia sprinkled the water on the shadows and that gave them different hue. All the shadows were shaped with the color they got.

"Oh! You came up at the right time. So you deserve the fair for this." Raflesia said looking to the tiny human colorful shadows. Saying this she again turned towards the Queen. "Your Highness, Albus is none other than the H...U...M...A...N- father of these babies." She purposely dragged the issue. On this, Romarin's sobs filled the cell.

"But Raflesia, how is it possible?" asked the Queen.

"They fooled us Your Highness; they played with your innocence." Raflesia gazed the Queen expecting her to stand-by. Queen blushed and uttered nothing.

"Your Highness." Annoyed Raflesia continued, "What are you waiting for?"

"Raflesia, err...I think, let this matter stand over for the present." dreadfully Said the Queen, she was hurt, yet hoped.

—

Hitherto, underneath there was tremendous movement in the pond beside the castle. Warrior sea horses and fishes were ascended suspect. Not only the eyesore dumps were loitering but now the vivid birds were also seen around the castle never been seen before.

—

"Please, your Highness! Mercy, on me, on my little ones, they have not even entered this world, I beg you please." Romarin said pathetically. On this, Raflesia moved towards her, "And what will you gift them? A shamefaced life for having culprit parents," Romarin got on her nerves but only she could do was to shed tears.

"Romarin, no mercy, you failed to prove your side, and you are a culprit." She said persistently. "A-N-D… Your Highness." turning towards the Queen, "You better know the RULES and CUSTOMS of our world", she bellowed as if she had an axe to grind. Despite of possessing all the qualities required to rule, Queen Olivia had never gained the confidence against Raflesia. Many had tried to unearth the truth behind this, but on the cost of their lives. Ultimately, the Queen feebly got up to announce.

"As per the RULES and CUSTOMS of our world, I Olivia-de-peace, order you maid, as Romarin-de-heal have failed to prove her innocence and she is a culprit, I order you to…"

"Your Highness." A new voice entered with a short woman, fair as snow, brown wavy hairs, and apt features with decisive look. She hurried towards the Queen, "I beg your pardon Highness, but before going to any conclusion p-l-e-a-s-e I beg you to reconsider your decision." that kindhearted woman paused for a while.

"As you know the R-u-l-e-s- of our world, we cannot punish anyone downtrodden." She lobbed a sharp, side-glance at Raflesia on her last words. [Erica, she was the preacher of Tulika and the only one to know the truth about Romarin and Albus.]

"Erica, you don't know who she is and what are those tiny shadows." Raflesia said.

"Uh…well, I came to know right now, but we cannot punish her without knowing the truth. Your Highness, how could we be so rude?"

Queen Olivia found her heart, saw Raflesia hopefully, but………….

"Whatever you say Erica, has no bearing on the subject in hand." Raflesia said annoyingly as she seemed to have the situation out of her hand.

Erica was shuddered.

"But Your Highness…" Yet she made a vigorous defensive attempt.

"Don't thrust your nose into my affairs." Raflesia cut her short.

Flustered Erica could not say anything further.

A sudden movement from the shadows fetched Raflesia's attention. They grew larger and larger and were about to join when, "Babies… My babies… N…. o… o….o...Raflesia, don't you do that," wailed Romarin as she found Raflesia approaching towards her little ones. She struggled to get free from the maid's clasp but the hold was tight. Erica did not stay calm, she spelled and formed a translucent hedge around the tiny shadows and stood beside them.

However, no one from the inner or outer space might dare to amend the Raflesia's malicious resolution right away. She found the way out; she spelled on her armlet which turned into a string and that covered the hedge crafted by Erica. Within no time the translucent hedge dissolved and the earth around the shadows and Erica broke down making the huge gap. Now they were standing on the island that was separated from all the sides. Moreover, there arose the hellhole from the huge gap. A slight moment was enough to throw them to get churned into the fire. Everyone there was baffled, and besides, Raflesia banged the rod.

—

It seemed a signal to the outer rooty creatures; they all got ready to have their part of share first. The wild twigs tried to thrust inside the window, but were pushed back forcibly. Nevertheless, they had to cross through the echelon pull out by the countless Butterflies around the vicinity of the castle.

—

Indoors, Raflesia approached towards her prey and leapt across the hellhole without falling into it.

"So then, how did you find my way?" she asked and chortled

mercilessly. Erica, who was covering the shadows, got displeased "you will have to pay for this, you heartless." She said irately.

"O! You daft you have welcomed a distress for you and your pets." Raflesia said getting on her nerves. Now she was ought to cause detriment. "Don't worry dear, I will set you aside to help Romarin." Saying this she turned back to the flank of the cell, saw Romarin sharply and move towards the throne. She bowed her head in front of the Queen and said "Your Highness, power me to conduct this matter and to wind up." Her determination did not let the Queen to refuse her, though the Queen wished. The Queen Olivia glazed at Romarin and Erica, as if requesting them to understand her feebleness.

Without waiting at Queen's consent Raflesia got up, turned towards the gloomy crook, and bellowed "O! Mighty powers of this world I Raflesia-de-rot, command you to appear, for Her Highness."

Not only the Queen but also even the powers could not snub her. Her utterance filled the cell with luminosity that beamed through the rod of gold having a seven-colored flower as the top and a small round mirror as its anther.

The beam of light enhanced the beauty of those charming little shadows. They were unable to remain motionless, which may lead them right away into the hellhole. Witty Erica bound them with one invisible cord so that Raflesia could not detect it, but awhile. Raflesia stoop before the golden rod, she held it and lifted it upright in the air. This led to the havoc among those present there. Romarin went to pieces when she saw this, even the Queen Olivia got scared but...

Raflesia did not gave up, she almost snarled,

 "Hocus-Pocus behold your Focus

　　Let the earth get shatter and

　　These hues get scattered."

Tremendous thunderclaps in the sky quakes everyone in and out of the doors. The unexplainable was ought to occur on Raflesia's hex. The golden rod swirling in the air moved towards the shadows. Erica trying to retort was caught by one of the ray passed by the rod and it threw her asides near the throne. The golden rod now went on moving swirling above and bitingly thrust deep into the midst of the island breaking it into pieces and leaving the flower fraction out.

The little shadows spring in the air at once and were just ready to drop into the hellhole but not, they hang on the strings appeared by the Erica's spell.

—

Meanwhile, the echelon pull out by Butterflies was cross over by the twigs, dumps seemed ecstatic to have the grand feast.

—

"E-r-i-c-a- look out! Save my children.' Romarin's scream drew every one's attention towards the movement noticed in the rod's upper part that remained out.

Rapidly, the rooty strings gripped the flower from behind. They bind each petal tightly and began to crush them. The crushed flower stretched itself to get release and while doing so...one by one the colors of the petals dripped out spreading all over. After making the flower colorless, the rooty strings released it by own and disappeared. This made Raflesia ecstatic, she spelled again and an elliptical inferno moved around the strings that had been holding the shadows for long; and cut them forcibly. Instead of harm, this proves to be of great rescue for them. Each of the string took the shadows across the hellhole. But they started slipping down owing to their wobbly hold. Romarin got the situation, so she wildly knocked the maid and rushed to their help. Erica too, tried to get the hold of anyone if she could and she got one of them.

Well, how can this be bearable by Raflesia? She saw this and using her hand as a wand, threw the magical spelled ball that hurt Romarin's belly and hit the Erica's hand that had almost pulled the little one up. She then immediately dropped the hold and the shadow fell down, as the others.

Romarin screamed in agony seeing her little ones getting into the hellhole. "Be within the foliage, if you live." Romarin shrieked not letting her hopes to collapse. On this, Erica spelled cloak-and-dagger and something followed the shadows in the hellhole.

After a while, the golden rod burst out from the mud and vanished. Everything rolled up as previous and it seemed nothing had happened unwanted.

After confirming the Situation, Raflesia left the cell, Queen Olivia and her maids had to go helpless. Wailing Romarin was taken behind the bars, poor Mum. "O! It is my entire fault! God please save them." She went on saying whiles the maid locked her in the dark lonely chamber in the basement. Yet Erica, not able to believe the aftermath, chased Raflesia.

The shadows descended in the different direction outside the castle. They had been saved by the armor formed by Erica's spell, but uncertain to slip away from the weird rooty creatures, which were already waiting to grab them.

They found themselves in front of the giant lively tree; it seemed they did not give ear to their Mum's advice so rushed far away from it and that proved dangerous… running far away they all thought of getting through out of this but……………

—

The fiend Raflesia, not willing to cease-fire splattered water from the jar on her skull-rod. The skull got lifted with the rooty strings. Raflesia touched a string and that string transformed into the peck of blood-curdling creature, a female monster with wings and hissing serpents for hair on her body. "Go get them." Raflesia further parted the creature from middle and came out several alike. She ordered them, "until don't turn up." They -the Gorgons, grinned hellishly.

Dither Erica rushed to act her part; she hole up into the dark and spelled folding her hand in a fist. When she opened her fingers, one by one, teeny-weeny creatures came out and she asked them to protect the shadows from Raflesia's strike. All the creatures were the spirit looked like fairies; they had colorful wings and a colored transparent body. They-the Nymphs, bowed themselves in front of Erica and flew away.

—

The chronicles resumed. The shadows were moving down at full pelt. The Gorgons found their prey and rushed towards them puckishly. As soon as they came near the shadows, the Nymphs attacked them. They got muddle up by a sudden attack through Nymphs.

Now fight began between these two. The formers were injured, but soon found the way; they stretch their side-wings and moved heaven and earth to crush the later ones, but could not.

By the time, the little ones managed to move out, but after going few steps ahead they shook in their shoes, the wild rooty creatures caught them... Suddenly, everything stopped for a while, the twigs swinging in the air swirled around as twister and all the shadows thrust into it...

This, the warrior saw, the Gorgons wanted the proof of their last breathe, so they plunge into the tornado and the Nymphs would not allow to end easily, so they too rushed in. Within no time, the typhoon stopped and everything with the shadows vanished, and after a while only a little flower bud hurl out. The evil won, as there was no sign of the shadows or the warriors.

The sun rose with the darker shades, mournfully. Erica, was stuck to the ground, the tears welled up in her eyes. Raflesia not satisfied, yet, fling the spell into the air towards her and the air around Erica getting wild began to slap her, bashing her finally to the grave. The iron bars of the dungeon fell open, the deadly creatures took unconscious Romarin out of the castle into the dark, and the Queen Olivia was forced to take off her crown to embellish on Raflesia, from thereafter.

Finally, Raflesia got relieved she found herself in high spirits, but who knew, what the future beholds for her? The colors of flowers fade away, except one…

A shadow, maybe the youngest one was too fearful to move so it found a place to hide itself in the hollow of a giant tree. It was the only untouched witness of the events that night. Early at the peep of the day, when everything seemed finished, it came out shilly-shally, but its part of monster remained alive and before the Gorgon tried to grab it, it ran and ran, followed by a Butterfly hiding among the bushes.

GANESH VISARJAN

[She goes running feverishly moving her head behind after every second, seems she was running from fear and maybe that followed her. Dressed in a turquoise blue blazer and align skirt with blood red inner. A blue necktie fastens with the red belt at her waist she, definitely looked like a schoolchild. She ran nonstop without failing to check behind. The drops of sweat flew down from her forehead to her long sharp nose and settled on her left cheek to wipe out with her long fair fingers. Her big dark brown eyes were afraid and trembling pink bow shaped lips were open to scream, but no one is there to hear her. What is she running for? Or who is chasing her?]

I am running on boulevard, exhausted. I looked back and shook for a while, a long dark all alone street, not even one to swear. I could not bear that long. Two teeny-weeny lights fetched me back; I followed it without reason. The lonely straight cul-de-sac covered with dark surroundings as if dying to grab you and you tend to run from it towards life.

Now it must have been almost an hour, to confirm I glanced at my wrist but not exactly I could see only ten minutes past 00-hrs. What is this? Only ten minutes have passed. Oh! It seems I am running for so…...long. I yearn to end as my patience and strength both are at an end. I was done up and eager to reach the dead end just like an athlete. However, the unexpected always happens; the distance was not ready to end.

Suddenly those teeny-weeny lights disappeared and I lost my aim- everything seemed foggy to me and…

"GANPATI BAPPA MORYA," Somebody screamed in my ear and sprinkled something over me. I forced my eyes to open wide. Jesus! What a fuss! A dark woman with her long hair open, big round black eyes with a penny sized red colored sticker in the middle of her forehead stuck between two longbow shaped eyebrows, was staring at me suspiciously. She carried an aluminum glass which made me realized that my face is still wet due to that glass of water. [I hope so]

"Get up, Herbriella Hey! What's up to you?" somebody else called me, with my name [I guess]. I saw a neither a fat nor a thin woman with short curly brown hair tied in a ponytail gazing me in surprise. Behind her, there were many girls and boys standing with the same look on their face. I wonder they were dressed like me.

"Hey, Herbriea, What happened?" a dark skin, curly haired girl came closer to me. Even I did not know why I was lying there. I just looked at her. She then raised her hand and helped me to get up. I wiped out my face and saw the woman who called my name. I sincerely tried to recognize her but in vain.

"Come on, don't you know me? I am Mrs. Rao; don't act silly. Get up fast." She realized my confusion; with a jerk, I remembered everything. Her familiar tone – always ready to evaluate the students especially me can never be forgotten. She is my Dorm warden. And now I recalled everything clearly.

We all had gathered here for the procession of the Lord Ganesha's deity immersion. Today was the last day of Ganesh Chaturthi i.e., Anant Chaturdashi – an Indian Festival celebrated for ten days; people invite Lord Ganesh in a statue form, worship them and immerse the idol of the Lord on the last day. The ceremony of immersion was yet to be carried out.

I saw Nanisha and Mouzami, my best friends, ready to pounce on me. As I moved towards them suddenly that goggle-eyed woman caught me again and said "Jadu-kada-jadu", she said in Marathi –an Indian Maharashtrian language. I was able to understand the language but not its meaning. On this, my friends came nearer to me and asked me the matter. I tried to recall and remembered about my race on boulevard, two bright lights, etc. but the question was how I was lying flat and nobody from my side noticed me, instead a stranger got me to say those tricky something absurd. I had many questions on my psyche, but of the essence was how? I asked myself, I started digging my memory. The stuff I found was more awful than that goggle-eyed woman was. I went to the starting point.

As it was an immersion day, our boarding school always takes part in Vai's sarvajanik Ganesh immersion that was four-five km., far from Panchgani. It takes half-n-hour to climb down, we have to walk all the way and this was the most enjoyable part that we all share together.

All students were grouped class wise in four rows. Students of Class first and second were ahead of all and were followed by third and fourth Class students. Then huge 11 feet tall idol of Ganesh was moving on the cart among the fifth and sixth class. They were playing lazim, including me, of course. I had always loved to play lazim, it boost my energy. At the last, the natives of Vai village followed Class seventh – ninth, teachers, and sirs. It seemed that whole village was out today. It looked like a carnival, with colors everywhere. I had always liked this festival; do not remember exactly, but my Mum use to tell me the stories of Lord Ganesh, Lord Shiva, Lord Hanuman and lot more. She was the great devotee of Lalbaugcha Raja in Mumbai. She uses to visit India to take his blessings once in a year, at any cost. May be because I have heard all this from my Mum, I feel proud to be a part of this procession.

Lord Ganesha's idol, 11 feet tall was in sitting position with four hands, two hands ahead, Left one holding a plate of Laddus [sweets] and giving blessings with the right one. The natives believed that Lord Ganesh liked the Laddus most, so they offer these Laddus to get his blessings.

An elephant faced God has a vast history in Indian mythology. This festival is among the most popularly celebrated Indian festival. They adorn an idol richly with the precious ornaments, jewels, gems, pearls and of course Golden yellow silk pitambari [cloth]. Ganesha is a God of wit, wealth and success and worshipped in each Hindu Religion initially. Were you going for an exam, an interview, or has any auspicious occasion, a wedding or an achievement, Lord Ganesha is worshipped first. So he is a king of Gods and that is why called Raja.

The serenity present in Ganesha's wide eyes enhanced his gorgeous look. While playing lazim I could not take away my eyes out of him. Whenever I look into his eyes, I feel him saying, "I am always there for you, don't worry, go ahead." All these I have heard from my Mum.

As I was busy playing lazim, I found some trouble in the first row that is among Class first students. Being a Good Samaritan, I had to see into the matter. Therefore, leaving the game in the midway, I went there.

Merletta was lying on the ground unconscious and the procession unaware of her was non-stop moving ahead. I rushed to stop them and took Merletta in my arms. All the students were shocked on my sudden arrival. Teachers and volunteers helped me to take Merletta aside below the giant banyan tree. This incident should not affect the procession, so it kept moving and they left one volunteer to help me... Soon we saw the procession passed far away from us. Only Lial and Veronica were the last to move on, but they stopped and came towards us, suddenly everything turned dark….gradually it became more and more dark. I could not see anything in pitch black; it felt like I was a lame duck.

Merletta was emotionally attached to me and we both had always enjoyed each other's company. She was the youngest close friend of mine. So I did not felt to join the procession without her. In spite of the dark, I was relieved to have Merletta in my arms, but I could not see that volunteer near us. I stretched my hands to feel her but she was nowhere. Oh! Where to find her? I was in a fix. I did not dare to search for her in such a haunted atmosphere. However, a terrible bushy noise from my backside forced me to get up at once. I turned back to see and could not stop screaming. A horrible creature was ready to grab me. I bet I had seen these kinds of creatures, only in Movies.

To my surprise, Merletta was not in my arms now; this made me more panic. I got up, ran, and ran towards life.

"Oops, so everything I owe to Veronica, you know why?" I told this to my chums, Nanisha and Mouzami.

"How is it possible?" said Mouzami frowning with her big round eyes. "Merletta was well throughout the procession and it was you who went aside, doesn't know why? But we didn't notice anything weird." Her big round face narrowed as she gave her statement.

"Then how come that whimsical lady come and says those words to me only." I protested.

"Come on, chill dudes, we are here to celebrate and not to argue, okay." Said Nanisha, sometimes she sounds to the point, but her fair skin always turned red whenever she has to express herself. Slim and trim face and stature proved her delicate than we.

Now an Idol of Lord Ganesh was being drawn into the Junnar Lake to be immersed. All the people including us said together.

"Ganpati Bappa Morya, Pudhchya warshi Lavkarya." Means "O, Lord you are great, please come back next year soon."

We all repeated several times. Meantime many native swimmers were immersing an Idol. None of the women or children was allowed that much deep in water, so we stayed far at the lake's bank. It felt amazing, when all the people get together forgetting their conflicts and enjoy together.

I saw Veronica not far from that goggle-eyed woman was on the other side of the crowd. Veronica was the only one I would not like to face today. Her fairest skin always brightened as she encounters me. Suddenly that woman said something to Veronica and glared at me.

Well, I wished I was not here, I tried to keep my sight apart from her, but she fetched me again. She started moving towards my side, as she came near the steps, she waved her hand towards me, and I thought I rock the crowd. Oops, she fell down on the steps, and before anyone from the crowd could hold her, she rolled down all the steps and fell into the lake. Soon one of the native jumped after her and within few minutes, that boy got her on the bank.

Some of the natives treated her to throw out the water that must have entered her body. Two-three women were airing her. All these worked out after a while. She opened her eyes and stared everyone, shuddery. All of them gathered around her. I heard somebody in the crowd saying that Merletta was the cause. I looked for Merletta, she, standing behind five-six teachers to my left was not at all aware of this. On the contrary, she asked about the matter and somebody told that as she ducked down to pick up her Prasad [sweet] which had fallen down, this woman unknowingly climbed on Merletta and fell down. Now the matter was cleared.

"Akka, oothaki, barr vataye na aata." A woman asked from the flock. This goggle-eyed woman was called as Akka and was asked to get up, if she felt better now then. She said nothing but her eyes moved hastily all around and…as it sighted me it stopped. She again raised her hand pointing towards me, now this was the limit. I felt several eyes on me with a question. I knew that question but the answer I could only expect from "Akka". So I moved ahead, sat down and asked her looking into her eyes what is the matter? Her weighty eyes forced her chops and as it opened, a dark fluid flew out from her mouth. Entire crowd there got shocked and moved back, even I tried to get far but, she hold me back; she hold my arm and tried to tell me something. Alas! She could not speak now, she lost her voice, it seemed. Moving vigorously here and there, she went on asking about her distress, but who can guess the reason? Even the people were on tenterhooks. It made us all to forget the celebration and instead worrying over, with which we students had never any bond.

Mrs. Julianne Brook, our headmistress with the management person, assured all the natives for the well-being of "Akka" in Hostel's hospital. She immediately arranged for the Doctor van and took her to the hospital. The crowd was almost scattered. Teachers asked us to get into our school buses. Everyone moved slothfully towards their respective bus. Walking heavy steps, I had to move, too.

Anyone can believe or not, but I deeply felt of having my nexus with all these chronicles. I remember many times I have come about the things that the people are afraid to think even. I have the brilliant mind, but found it difficult to tackle the weird dreams I see with my open eyes. Mum had always called me little magician and I took it in, but the feel I used to feel was instead dreadful than magical.

As I was moving pensively, something flashed on the ground; it was shining very brightly. As I picked that thing, it stopped shining and found it having some scratches too. Oh! What a stupid of me, it was just a piece of scalene stone; I need to throw it. I would have definitely pitched it, unless it had not blazed again. It demanded a second thought, so I skinned it within my pocket. Possibly, it may have some magic; I thought.

"This is what, I don't like" hard-nosed Mouzami raised my hairs.

"What?" I asked stepping into the bus.

"Look, you said because of Veronica and Lial you got into the scene, right?" I nodded.

"But I have a doubt." Saying she looked for comfortable seat.

"See" she continued as we parked ourselves, "Veronica and Lial than Niyati-volunteer and Merletta? Why does Merletta? She was in your lap, right. Then she cannot be in your concern." Still postmortem was not finished.

"Hey, friends have this," offered Nanisha raising her hand with a packet of "Namkeen" branded roasted nuts. I was about to have some, but Mouzami plug up my heave hand giving severe look to Nanisha.

"As you say you fainted because of Veronica then why did not you have conscious because of Merletta?" Mouzami said, expert in expanding the issue to the conclusion.

"Dear Herbriella, this is the side-effects of too much of Harry Potter, Spidy, Narnia and what else." Nanisha said giving Mouzami her hand. [Everyone knew my magic mania. Oh! I always wished my affiliation with magic]

Well, these were my dudes, they disagree to my suspect, and yes, these were my best Langotia friends - infancy friends.

"So now confirmed, it was my Hallucination, nothing to do with the present right?" I said putting my tools down.

They agreed and we arrived at our hostel's gate.

<u>Chap- 3</u>

<u>The Silhouette</u>

Mouzami Grazier is a student of class-4 from South Africa and Nanisha Scrivener from Los Angeles, U.S.A. same class. They both a year younger to me, are the only my best friends trusting me.

I, Herbriella Gold, am studying in class-5- Minerva boarding school-Panchgani-India and came from Canada. My Mum- Mrs. Kathy Gold, admitted me in this hostel four years back when she passed away. She wanted me to stay in India. Initially, she was from London and shifted to Canada before my arrival in this world. She was a Teacher of Human Psychology teaching in City School of Canada.

It was my birthday- 25th October, when we both stayed in Hotel for two days in Mahabaleshwar. Mahabaleshwar- one of the renowned hill stations of Maharashtra and Panchgani, situated at the peak of ranges was a heaven famous for bearing many excellent, nifty boarding schools. Next day we got finished all legal formalities required for my admission in Minerva Boarding School one of the best. My Mum then went to Kutch towards north west of India, may be for some kind of work. She did not tell me, as though I was not of that age to understand. However, later I got it when she had called for me. It was the third day of December, in the same Hotel, one of my Dorm wardens took me to see her.

My Mum, a tall personality, fair very fair, grey eyed, curly long brown hair, alike to a fairy. She had dimpled smile for which I have always longed and tried many possibilities to carve in mine, though not natural, but failed. Yet, she was the cutest with those dimples and I always tried to see them frequently. Today also I tried, but her aggrieve, eyes covered it.

She is suffering from any disease,

which I came to know today. Her eyes rolled down from my eyes to lip, maybe she wished me to react, but I could not. Well, I could not even ask her about her trip to Kutch, but she told me herself, taking my hand into hers. "Herbie" she uses to call me that, "I know you must be wondering that till, now, where was I, and she paused for a while, "I had gone to keep my promise that I made you to get that you had insisted, Herbie."

"Then, where is he, Mum." I was overjoyed to welcome my biggest gift ever to this day. The gift I had demanded was beyond all the fancies of this world, or it was the part of my world to accompany my Mum, and of course me. I felt excited.

"Sorry, dear I failed to keep my word." the gruff voice coughed, she was crying.

"Don't worry mummy, I don't want anything, I will never ask for anything, but please don't cry, I want you." I was definitely disappointed but I had never liked to see my Mum crying as she often, so I wiped her eyes. She pulled me closer to rest on her stomach and went on crying much than before. She made her hold tight and patting my back she said, "Better luck next time, you, my strong little magician will find him anyway, I know." she cheered me up.

"Mum, can I stay with you tonight." I was clear with my Hostel's rule, still I hoped.

"Well…" she indecisively looked on Mrs. Rao, my warden. She than asked my Mum to take Headmistress permission. In addition, after a while I was allowed to be with my Mum for one night.

That whole night I found even more caring, more gentleness, yet she went on weighting me on being stronger, and at the next moment, she insists me not to puzzle with grownups talk- just watch out my studies and so on. One more thing I found in her eyes that night, even if she did not reveal, it was a Fear. She behaved impatiently that whole night.

"What's the matter Mum, are you afraid of something?" she stared me helplessly.

I got my answer after two days. I was brought again to see her, but this time to her funeral. I could not cry, I could not understand my own feelings itself. Mrs. Julianne Brook buried my face in her overcoat taking me closer.

Fear, yes it was that fear of being away from me- forever. Now I feared to be here without her, without my Mum. Can you just imagine how one can survive without one's life?

Nevertheless, Mrs. Brook did never lurch me. She always reminded me of my Mum's belief in me. How can I ever forget her belief of being my magician and the gift that she failed and asked me to help myself? These red pages, though written in my diary, which I started writing on the same day, I had never felt a need to go through it, it's all in my heart.

"Herbriea" Mouzami pulled me out of my memories. "You said your father lived here, right? She asked.

"Here-where" I asked.

"Obviously, I am talking about this country, India, not this Hostel, duffer." She liked to tease. Without waiting for my reply, "So he was an Indian, right." She guessed.

"Come to the point." I was annoyed.

"Don't mind, that's why , I guess, you look like Anglo-Indian, see this straight black hair, Indian fair skin, dark brown eyes, long sharp nose and …and …a nut like…" saying this she went far from me.

"Now you're finished." I chased her and we moved around Nanisha.

"Like whom you called me a nut?" I asked while trying to hold her.

"Oh! I don't think your parents were nuts." She said jestingly.

"Then tell me, Mouzami." I again asked taking her hold, finally.

"Okay…Okay…listen…you are like George, I have always seen him flicking the books in the library and half the time pondering on …like you." "…though being Veronica's best friend, he looks pull towards you all the time, isn't it?" she hoped my consent.

"No way, ugh..." I pretended to be nonchalant, in fact, she was right. George always tried to converse with me, though he knew sure to bear Veronica's fury.

"Come on dudes, its break-fast time, and hurry, don't get stuck." Nanisha said breaking our argument.

"We'll catch you in the dining hall." Mouzami said waiting for the chance to be away from me and they went to their room.

I hardly wiped my thoughts and went for a bath. Within no time, I got, ready to step down. My room was on third floor, last from the staircase. We were six to share one room. There were five rooms on each floor and four floors in each six buildings. Our dining hall was spread in vast, spacious land next to our playground build up in dome like shape with bamboo roofs. The small bushes, yellow blossoms, Lily, orchids and many flowers, surrounded it.

I turned towards the dining hall, but the Veronica's presence at the gate stopped me to proceed. She was the peace less person on the earth, always trying to embarrass me with her nuisances. She is two year elder to me. From the day she had come here, does not leave any single, chance to harass me. She is the only child of her parents and so is the reason she is here. We study in same class. She thought her two inches more height than I allowed her to harass me and I must obey her. Anyway, her spiral curly hairs like her features proved her curly in nature, too. Her beaky nose always tried to get into my way unreasonably.

I was sure to get something new from her. As I went near the entrance, she blocked my way with the help of her two friends Pinky and Chinky. There were few more fellows behind them.

"H...e...y, you dunce, now happy to play your turn?" she started.

"What you are talking about?"

"It's easy to turn down, but it was you for whom 'Akka' has to hospitalize, in fact it is always you for all the miseries around." She said grudgingly. I set off from there when she again held me to threaten. "You ought to fear me. BEWARE, I'll watch you." "Watch ye, watch ye." her hopeless fellows joined her.

I tried to control myself as I had promised my dudes, unless I had showed her my turn. Mouzami and Nanisha started gulping as I reached there.

"Why late?" asked Mouzami taking a bite of toast-sandwich.

"Yes, I am the cause for 'Akka's…"I was ready to burst out of anger, but Nanisha held me.

"She's crack, don't take her in." she said. They had always known the cause.

"I'll try; she swears to watch me, always." I said sadly just staring my plate; it was full as such my heart with Veronica's attitude towards me. I had never thought of hurting her, but she would always upset the apple cart; don't know why?

"OA…TERI" suddenly we heard Kamaljeet Kaur of my class who just clash with the crockery beside Veronica's chair and unknowingly knocked Veronica causing her to tumble down dropping all the cuisine over her from the served plate. It seemed to be the hilarious accident for all of us and for me it was 'Tit for Tat' too. Unable to bear this insult, Veronica left her breakfast and dining hall leaving the curses and abuses behind. Within no seconds, the hall turned into the laughing club and the relishing stopped only when Mr. Jayant Patel, the catering in charge bellowed on us to leave the place soon. This incident put my stomach into effect, and I felt hungry.

At 9.30 a.m., our first lecture was to start and we had only 15 minutes left, so we finished our breakfast and rushed to our dormitory to get ready.

While stepping down for the school as I passed by the corridor I again found that gleaming tile stone lying on the floor. When I bend down to pick it up, I felt something scurried by me. Immediately I got up, but could not find anything. Well, as it was getting late, I did not wish to waste more time. I passed away the corridor and just had a step down; I felt something to my left side again. I stopped to see it properly; it was not so clear, but something linger few steps upstairs. Owing to dull corner, it was not visible but… then, I don't know how I dare to step up. I had just climbed up, when those two teeny-weeny lights shine and shiver me…

"What ale you doing hele, Helbliella?" A very sweet timid interruption was enough for those lights to disappear. Oh! Misfate, I missed it.

"Ale you not getting late? Come, we will go togethle to the school" said Merletta. She was unable to pronounce the letter 'R' that made her sweeter. All this happened just in a fluke, no reason to blame her. We together headed towards the school.

I was late again. Mrs. Rienzi was not at all surprised on my arrival. Might had thought, it is better late than never. As though, she knew the yesterday's incident, she did not utter a word. I politely said "sorry" and took my seat. She was our class teacher taking History and English subjects.

I was still pensive when she asked me "Yes Herbriella, tell me the meaning of "Mummification." A lesson on World's Tradition and Customs- Egypt, was taught a day before yesterday and today we were supposed to give the summary by-heart, this I remembered just now. I was helpless. I got up and tried to answer which I doubt to be correct yet, I said, "Over many centuries, the ancient Egyptians developed a method of preserving bodies, so they could remain life like. Today we call this process "Mummification." However, to my surprise it was the correct answer. Mrs. Rienzi was impressed, asked me to sit and continued with her further explanation. History and English were my favorite subjects and so was Mrs. Rienzi.

During her explanation, I started pondering once again. Those teeny-weeny lights were not leaving my mind. I wonder, it was reminding me of something, I guessed, I thought little bit deeper and those lights lit up my mind. I had seen the same yesterday. Oh! I got it now; it was enough for my chums to believe. "Trin…n…n" babble forced me to leave my thoughts out and relax, as it was a break for twenty minutes.

Some of the students went out and some remained in the class only. I saw Mouzami and Nanisha coming to me. Their classroom was on the same floor, so we used to spend more of our time together. I told them about the lights, they said it might be my illusion.

Discussing about this we went up to terrace, we often go there since the original keys were with us, otherwise it was a forbidden area due to a reason. Few months back as I was going upstairs, suddenly Lalit the former caretaker bump into me hurrying from the terrace and the keys were dropped on the floor. He then rushed down without bothering the keys. As there was nobody to take care of I picked the keys and thought to return them back later. However, I need not as Thomas was made in charge thereafter and the terrace was locked for all the students owing to the mishap occurred. And I remembered Lalit's scared face, sweating throughout, and his fearful wide eyes proving to have seen something dreadful. We had tried our best to find about the mishap, but the teachers were very sharp to let out the fact. So then, we three decided not to return these keys and find out the matter. Since then we became the only regular visitor of this place, but had never come by anything weird. Mouzami shut the door as soon as we got in.

"What do you think of all those stuff?" Nanisha asked.

"Crap, I don't believe, what about you?" Mouzami passed it to me.

"Well, good is always followed by bad and I think I feel it nowadays." I tried to explain them.

"Come on, we are talking about those rumors spread for this scope."

Mouzami would never believe the unseen facts.

We lighten up while viewing the scene downward. Many of the students were outside the building, some were chatting with friends, some having late breakfast and some little ones playing hide and seek. We enjoyed watching such scenes from so much height so we use to come here though not allowed. Hide and Seek game always attracted me; it reminded me of my days with my Mum. I was so engrossed that I did not hear the school bell rang for our next class.

"Let's go, time's up." Nanisha said.

I turned my face from the sight downwards but my eyes could not, I saw those lights again behind the small bushes as if hiding from others but trying not to get far- off my sight.

"Hold back" I screamed, holding Mouzami arm, "Look there." I pointed towards the bushes.

"Where? What? We can't see anything!" asked Nanisha, leaning forward to see.

"See properly behind those tiny twigs, it is like two lights… and" my eyes *slipped down and...*

"Oh! And something black… oh no, it's a black structure… I think it is really a human; wrapped in full black robes from top to bottom. Only its teeny-weeny eyes are seen. O! I said this. O yeah, I see the same one, these days. So those were the eyes instead of lights and I found them starring me." I went on blabbering while my friends dragged me down. They believed it was my illusion and said that we need to talk on this later.

I entered my class and what I saw, Veronica with her two friends followed by Hindi teacher, looked ready to blast a bomb.

Mrs.Shakuntala Chaturvedi stepped forward with a question. "Where were you?" I could not reply.

"Herbriella, you are late for ten minutes. Tell me the reason." She yelled.

"I was in fresh room," these words randomly flew out of my mouth.

Veronica's face beamed with her vicious smile, as if she has revealed my truth and she proved it further.

'Ma'am' asked me to see her after school hours and allowed me to sit. Hindi subject was not difficult for me but today, whatever Mrs. Chaturvedi was teaching was going hay way. I was just physically in the class; mentally I was running after several incidents occurred recently. Veronica, as I knew was waiting for the chance harass me and that she did. She caught me as soon as the class was over. "So dummy, wat dyou think you'll get in supper? Any guesses? Hahaha…" And her fans followed her. I knew what she meant, so I kept nervously mum. However, she did not stop at this. She instead looked deeply into my eyes and said aloud "YOU can't go anywhere out of my sight." I was stunned for a while. She continued, "I'll always have a watch on you. And now you listen, dummy…" Suddenly, what happened that I got very furious and shouted, "ENOUGH, stop calling me names for you will find that two can play at that game." I was shivering like never before. Finding something unexpected, all the students in the class gathered around us. My sea changes shocked Veronica, but she immediately controlled herself and ferociously held my neck. I prevented myself by pushing her with hands. She made her hold very tight and I just kicked in her thighs with my knees. That proved very strong, she left me for few seconds but again came back. I was now ready in karate pose and as she came near, I hit in the air with my leg and she came closest to give me returns. That singled moment, Kamaljeet gave me her hand unknowingly by entangling her foot with veronica's when she was demonstrating few physical exercises in front of her group that had been taught yesterday and that single moment, our Math's teacher entered the class, saw our quarrel and took all the three of us to Headmistress office. She herself did not ask us anything and when Kamaljeet tried to tell her, she was not ready to listen anything on our side. I really felt sorry for Kamaljeet; she was unnecessarily dragged with us. But, it was funny to find her messed up with Veronica, always.

Headmistress had gone out for some job, we were asked to wait. After few minutes, Mrs. Julianne Brook, our headmistress entered with her all-time smiling face, today it was shining also. She surprisingly asked us about the matter. Mrs. Dale Mackerel narrated the whole story. On this, Mrs. Brook gave me a deep look as if not believing my part. She thought of something and then asked Mrs. Mackerel to cut off ten-ten points from our respective house, each. Then she asked Mrs. Mackerel to stay and three of us to leave. Veronica did not look ashamed; instead she held Kamaljeet as we came out of the office and warned her not to come into her way again. Innocent Kamaljeet went to her class with the utmost confusion. Well, she always get into trouble because of her jumble nature, but what about me? Anyway, I set off with the thought of Mrs. Brook. I found a different spark in her eyes; she was looking, charming today.

After my Mum's death, Mrs. Brook was the person to take my responsibility. I had always found everything from her, which I would have expected from my Mum. Mrs. Brook has round face with high cheekbones, round watery grey eyes, her broad shoulders showed her the most reliable person ever. She lived in her row house with her husband and only lame daughter of double of my age. She was a very perky and kind-hearted person. I always have a thought, why such an injustice to such kindness.

After the Mathematics and English dual class, a bell rang for a long break of 45 minutes. I moved towards canteen. It was now my turn to wait for my chums. I was eagerly waiting to tell them everything. My eyes were on the door and suddenly I saw that black structure loitering outside the canteen. I wonder was he invisible to others as nobody noticed him. Somehow, Jolting I followed it.

Refulgent climate suddenly changed and an overcast sky pissed down. I step out to confirm whether my illusion or what? Nevertheless, I found …every … thing…in the surrounding, turning dark. Under the roaring thunder, only I could see was that teeny-weeny eyes. The eyes with the human figure moved ahead and without bothering my clothes, I followed it. It was leading me ahead n ahead and moving just few steps, it jibbed, turned back, gave me a deep look. Ah! Those eyes were now clearly seen, blue transparent eyes. Suddenly, that silhouette which was not actually, raised its arm pointing towards the sky. I could not understand about the darkness that was surrounding me, whereas the sky was still shining with the blue tinge. And suddenly there was a movement in there. The silver clouds moved aside highlighting the huge structure as if revealing the hidden. It looked like a daydream. There was an orchard full of fruit bearing trees, innumerable flowers of different colors. And there spread out the red carpet lying at my feet. I was a bit confused when the orchard, to my surprise, took a jerk; the trees on the, either side drew back giving me the midway to pass through it. Without thinking further I walked through it and reached in front of an amazing huge pinkish-brown palace having several windows on each floor, crafted in a specific motif with dome shaped, roof. Suddenly I saw some words written boldly covering the whole palace. It was Hindi language with many signs and symbols along with. I thought, I could, so I tried to read it…

"Oh! Hi!" again the sweet voice interrupted me. It was Merletta flashing a torch on me. I was then hanging on the top of a giant banyan tree, holding a top most branch and instead of red; there was a green carpet of leaves spread all around. That palace, an orchard, flowers… nothing was found there.

"Solly, I came hele in sealch of my school badge, have you seen anywhele? Merletta asked.

"Hey, you dunce." Veronica found us. "How come both of you are here?

O! Teaching her your way, right? I told you so; you can't go out of my sight, never."

I was not in a state of answering her, as the skies brightness spread around me and my eyes went on shutting, which made my balance loose, and I fell down, everything seemed fuzzy to me and…

I found me in boarding's hospital with Nurse Mrs. Moore. At the first, I scanned myself and found no fracture or bandage in any of my body parts…oh good! Then I tried to feel the pain if I had developed any internal injury, but nothing was found. Thank Jesus!

"What? Don't be so happy." Mrs. Moore's words realized me that she had been waiting for me to come round might for long. The beds parallel to mine being empty, means that only I had been the lucky to take a rest.

"Thank your friend who has saved you from falling down straight on the ground. If she wasn't there you wouldn't have been able to open your eyes again." She said pouring liquid in the cup from the bottle labeled as 'Mercury chrome'.

"Oh no!" I got a bit scared.

"What!"

"I mean…My friend... Whom...But my chums were not there and Merletta…I don't think she could…she is too small to carry me." I was surprised.

"I know. It wasn't Melta that was another girl… of your class … well whats her name ve...ver... nca"

"Veronica" I helped her.

"Yes…yes that only girl…"

"Don't tell me…it's…its impossible…I don't believe."

"Why…why you can't? Such a nice…"

"NO she isn't. Actually speaking only because of her, I fell down." My tone increased.

"No you didn't."

"Okay, but I was going to and whatever she has done is just to prove. . ."
'Prove What?"

"Leave it" and I thought to better close this disagreement.

"Why you are messing up yourself, my child." Mrs. Moore said handing me a cup of medicine. I took it with my shivering hand or it shiver after I held the cup.

"Oh! Come on, don't you trust me?" She understood my hesitation and held the bottle from which she has given me the medicine. "I removed the tag that was worn -out and labeled it wrong… of course, by mistake." Her voice rose to prove herself. Well there was no other option than to drink the medicine in a sip. I had it with a sour feeling but it gave a better feel to my body. This was the unbeatable true love that Mrs. Moore has had always for us. She was the most experienced person in the Hostel. Though being retired from the school's clerical work, she was entrusted to look after sick pupils in the hospital. Her gentle caring nature has had always proved supreme on her ugly features. Unaware of her nature many had many times ignored her, but she did never complain or ill-treated anyone. "Hebiea" she often forgot my name, in fact everyone's, but I liked it, "Rosemary will be anytime here and I think she is able to help you out your complications." Saliva inside my mouth got bitter at the thought of Dr. Rosemary Teasel. The nerves inside my head started entangling, giving me severe headache. Dr. Rosemary was psychiatric and that proves I am sick and no way connected to magic world. I just closed my eyes maybe I could overlook this one.

I thought the recent incidents were, inter-connected with one another. The silhouette was trying to show me something. However, who was that? Moreover, why he chooses me, why not Veronica? [I could not think this happening to my chums.] I cannot even share this with others, or else I will be the next abnormal patient of Dr. Rosemary. Oh no, I got

Dr. Teasel added to my mental life too.

Suddenly someone's hasty footfalls drew my attention towards the door and it opened with my increased heartbeats.

"Oh! You scared me." I felt relieved.

"Instead, you scared us," Mouzami and Nanisha came inside caringly.

"What on the earth helped you to climb that giant tree, you are hot today." Mouzami asked dancing her eyes.

"O, amazing, without touching how can you tell she is hot." Nanisha said this touching me.

"Oh! Nani, I am talking about the rumors being discussed in our school. Is it clear now?" Mouzami explained her. This cheered me, as it was our routine chore.

They heard me patiently and I showed them the stones I had found. Yet they thought it was my magic mania. They asked me to see the doctor. This annoyed me and I started arguing, "…that wasn't any illusion, I am not crazy to see that now and then."

"Shhh... Girls!" Mrs. Moore asked us to keep peace.

Nanisha followed her cogently and whispered, "We trust you Herbriea. But what's harm to see the doctor once."

"And anyhow you have to, as you are the only hope on which Mr.Apte can rely." Mouzami changed the topic. Mrs. Moore moved around my bed doing her routine medical chores and giving her consent to my chums.

"And this time your football match is with whom, you know; house-Green you better know that."

"You are right, my present needs me. Don't worry I'll be all right soon." At least I can do this for their hopes.

"So get repaired fast and be prepared, your folks need you." Saying this they wrote a GWS note on my wrist as they were the only my kith and kin.

Their exit reminded me of my today's class that I would miss. They both left my room and I was left with my queries and the burden of my encounter with Dr. Teasel.

Chap-4

Foot Ball Match

I hoped for the bright sunny day and it was. All the other students, teachers, other spectators in the audience were packed out and ready to view the performance of their best player and cheer up for him or HER. Yes, today's match was held among GIRLS and Boys of the same class, i.e. 5-A and 5-B.

I was allowed to play after completing my divine treatment i.e., Pranayam, mental exercises, Yoga and Dr. Teasel even used 'Touch Therapy' on me- her special treatment. According to her, I was now fit to participate in the match. She prescribed me the mental-exercise regularly.

Players of both the teams were on the ground, warming up themselves, few minutes remained to start the game.

Hazel, Jyoti, Aayushi, Marisha, Emma, Celina, Simi, Raveena, Betty, and last but not the least Veronica, yes she was good at this, Oh! Thank Jesus! These were my team players-House-Red.

We all were dressed in white sports uniform, divided skirt, 4 inches above the knee, with red and white stripped waist belt and hair belt, sports shoes and with a strong belief on our nose enough to win.

Class 5-B, our rival team still today reminded me of our last year's match with House-Yellow-Girls team. We had shoddily defeated them. Nevertheless, today was the different scene; George was the captain of House-Green. He was the bloody best player sincerely appreciated by everyone. This made us nervous at least once.

Since 4 years our team being a winner, this year our match was fixed with the boy's team. However, this time rather being a healthy competition, it was going to be a real rival competition.

Among the boys team, STD 5th-B-boys were the best players. Rick and

Ronak were defenders, Stephen-a goalkeeper; Smitesh, Hemal, Rustin, Heath, Darwin and Philip were their mid-fielders. Only Vrajesh and George to strike the goal but because of their foot-to-foot tactics they may prove heavy. Yet, they knew their today's competition to be stone hard. "Herbriella…" Mr. Apte hurriedly came near me. "Look, I know you are not well, but I still know you are the only one reliable. Don't take too much of stress and…" saying this he took me aside, after a while, my other team players also joined us.

"Hey, Herbriella!" a loud scream was heard from the audience. Everyone turned to see him. That native was holding a board of Mara Dona's picture and was pointing towards me. This made many in the audience to cheer up loudly. Now this was much more than enough for our team to boost up our spirits. I was pleasantly embarrassed and it lowered down the stress of critiques. Not only the whole school, but also some natives were present to view today's interesting match, of course, that made us special.

First bell rang to stop our movement, second to be alert and third to start. For the last time, I viewed, everything was perfect, my player's position and mine. Starting from the net- Betty was at goalkeepers' position, Hazel, Jyoti, Emma and Simi at defenders position followed by 3 mid-fielders- Aayushi, Celina and Raveena. Lastly, Marisha, Veronica and me, ready to strike a goal.

I selected left side of the pitch, as it was resolved. I breathe long, closed my eyes and recalled the Quidditch game in Harry Potter. I had always thought of playing a Broomball like Quidditch instead of Football, but unfortunately, we have no powers. How it would be amazing to hit the ball not by foot and by broom and just flew away after every strike, rather trying to recollect breathe to fill the lungs hastily. Nevertheless, all these are book's stuff, not of real life, isn't it?

Third bell rang, to make us start; we gird up our loins. As soon as I kicked the ball, George grabbed it and kicked it again towards his side. It was then bounced in the air by Rustin. This turned out to be strong. Celina, pinched it quickly, but it was then carried forward by Smitesh already present there. Emma, our best defender snatched the ball and dogged it towards me. However, Vrajesh the rivals striker, tried to grab it. Not letting him, I kicked the ball swiftly and passed it towards Marisha running along. Meantime, the ball was passed to Veronica as I reached the first line.

After badly defeating the girls of House Yellow, they were very disappointed. So, consoled and convinced by their coach to bore away this year. Moreover, to prove our ability, our coach Mr. Shrikant Apte accepted their challenge. He prepared and encouraged us both physically and mentally to win against class 5-Boys, House-Green. Therefore, this was the reason of today's match being held among the Boys and the Girls.

Darwin and Philip moved heaven and earth to grab the ball from Veronica and me. They succeeded and by dodging, passed it towards George, present near the net. He immediately kicked the ball against the net but Betty racked herself and defended their strike smartly. "WOW! Hats off, Betty." I shouted. The sound of cheers and claps helped us to continue energetically.

It was again our turn to hold the strike and the firebrand Ronak to strike. Until then it was not difficult to cope with these boys, but equal footing was the most important and further I was not sure.

We had been asked to pay more heed on defending, as it seemed difficult to top. Mr.Apte said, "No matter you flunk, it is their victory that matter." So we were advised to boost up our defender's state.

Hither and thither went the ball until it reached to Hazel, but the wrathful Hemal could not bear this and he passed it trying his best and George caught the ball, but again it was filched by chirpy Jyoti. She passed it towards me; I kicked it against the net, an unexpected blow towards Stephen was hardly accepted by him, so was about to miss…but from where that crackpot Lial arrived and defended bravely. A louder cheer this time was heard.

Even the House Green seemed to come around with us, at defending, though not getting through. The scoreboard showed 0-0 position.

Now I asked Marisha to defend the strike, to this Veronica, ferociously, stepped forward, pushing Marisha aside and stood as a veteran. This did irritate Marisha.

"Unless we pull together we cannot succeed." Instead of Veronica, I told this looking on her.

Veronica was definitely a good striker; this does not proved Marisha an inch down. She had the same peach. My advice was thrown away upon Veronica, as she stuck to her position. From her attitude, it was clear that she wants to pay off old scores. Same attitude I saw in Lial, as he kicked the ball high in the air. He was the best friend of Veronica. Might be this was the cause I wonder.

Within no second, a ball was surrendered by full back. I rushed full tilt and kicked the ball against the net but Rick defended and his pass was caught by Ronak then to Rustin- Smitesh- Hemal and so on, this way it went on for at least five-six minutes. By this time, we have all tried enough to break their girdle, but could not. I felt Raveena gazing at me, being fuddled. I showed her my middle finger, as such she was waiting for this, she smirk and ducked into the girdle to seize the ball, and finally she earned it from Vrajesh. This was then strongly kicked and thrown far away by Aayushi. Simi caught it and dodged it with Celina. They passed it to Veronica. Marisha, did try to dodge with Veronica, she allowed her. They were at fair play and succeeded to bring the ball near the net, though rivals interrupted them.

Coming nearest to the aim, Veronica started dodging the ball alone. This was risky, so everyone, including Mr.Apte advised her to leave out. This made no difference in her intention. She continued and as she came near the net, she kicked the ball. At last, all of us thought of a goal, but it never happens that our wishes are just fulfilled. Before, the ball could reach and hit the net; George in turn kicked it. I did not allow it to go far and passed towards Marisha. She kicked it strongly against the net but Stephen had an enough time to defend it.

"Huh! Misfate!" and we felt Goose bumps with the buzzing of bell saying 'time's up.'

With the end of 0-0 score first round of 45 minutes was over, break of 30 minutes followed by second round. Players of both the team shake their hands and walked to their changing rooms to loud cheers, and howl both. Anyway, this is only the game; we had to be a sportsman, actually.

"Well done, Champs," Mr.Apte patted us as we entered our changing room.

"But sir, we didn't gain." I thought of reminding him or for the time I felt like a looser.

"Doesn't matter, as you didn't let them, too."

"Now pay attention." Mr.Apte said opening his mind filled with too many tricks for winning the game. As we were busy discussing the tactics to be used on the field further, Mouzami and Nanisha turned up.

"Hi! friends" said Mouzami frantically.

"Hi! How was that?" I had always welcomed their opinion.

"Well, unexpected." Nanisha replied.

"Wait, be here and you'll figure out yourself." We continued with our training and now we were ready to play both the way. My chums didn't leave me throughout this.

"Crap, do you think you'll get through with this." I told you so Mouzami would ever believe without marks.

"Oh! So, now you will train us, right." Veronica had heard us.

"What's your problem, don't start again, you've already let us down." I could not stop pointing her.

"WHAT! You are blaming me. HOW DARE YOU?" she went on the rampage.

"Yes, if you'd have let the pass to Marisha, then we could have gained at least one goal." I reproved her. This made her more furious.

"Darn you" she hold my arm, I was prepared this time, but before I could kick her.

"Girls! What's up? Why?" and we were caught.

"This will sap your strength; you need it on the field." Veronica released me, but stayed tuned with my sight. We both apologized to Mr.Apte and proceeded out. On the midway, Veronica held me back, and threatened me, "Darn you, wat you said, you'll've to eat your words." Mr.Apte could not watch this, perhaps he left before us. Nevertheless, this did not go out of my chum's sight.

We were well instructed before the game started, so were hoped not at fault. Veronica was yet, fretted. A loud cheer from the spectators raised our spirits. We got back on form.

It had always poured down during our match; today was the same. Clouds were getting dark and any moment we might be drenched, it seemed. We enjoy playing in wetly pitch; obviously, it had been our practice, since last four years.

I kicked the ball high in the air and ran towards left. Veronica moved indolently and let the pass go towards George. I had to run long to save the ball going into their grip. Oh! Thank Jesus! Aayushi accomplished my wish. She snatched the ball from, now with Hemal and carried forward. Meanwhile, I reached nearer to the spot. In spite, of being followed by the rivals, Aayushi, succeeded to bring the ball near the net. It was then passed to Marisha to kick.

Suddenly, the climate changed as it was hoped, to pour down; instead, a blow of hot wind touched everyone. Holding those black clouds, a sky turned to dark greenish, seen never before, and with its tremendous thunder claps and hot stormy wind it seemed to portend something evil. However, we continued, Marisha's foot lifted to kick the ball, remained in the air. Instead veronica kicked it towards the rivals, and I ran to grab it. I almost brought the ball nearest to the net and was about to kick, *but suddenly there was a blackout in front of my eyes, nothing was visible except darkness. Nor was the noise audible, it seemed that I was left alone on the ground. I wiped my eyes several times and then gradually the darkness faded into grayish fog. After a while the fog too was fading away. I moved my head to view little more and saw a greenish smoke in the midst of the net. What's that? It seems that the fog that was filled in my eyes turned into the smoke and set itself in the net changing its color. I shuddered for a while, and pulled back my kick. In spite of the dark clouds, the wind passed away was burning like hell.*

"Herbriella… help me… please… help me out…" The voice came from the midst of the net. Somebody needs my help but it was not seen. I looked around, everywhere but only the smoke was fetching my focus each time. Is that smoke speaking to me? Oh yes! Then is it going to turn into human being when I will touch it like magic? Might be! Am I into the magical world? Oh yes! It's the thing I had always awaited and might I get the way towards my gift. The magical thoughts came to my mind and I was then randomly drawn towards it. Ball was then left aside; I went on and on until I saw that smoke whirling, twisting, itself and formed in a giant tree- a huge, but ugly tree. Well, the magic again. It raised its branchy hand to help me in. I would not have touched it if I knew it would burst and brownie dull leaves will come out to spread far and near. It horrified me; suddenly, my knees and calf started shivering and I was already sweltered. To find the way out of it, I expectantly, turn towards spectators' side, but…wait, what's this? Instead of the people, the thick bushes were found,

none of my friends, no teachers, no players on the field and not the single sign of humankind round the whole scope but I found someone, yes, only the Merletta was sitting beside a bush. I was relieved to see, at least, Merletta was there to support me. I summoned her in a hope to help me out, but she, instead of replying, went on glaring in the midst of the net. Thank Jesus; I got at least, one to my side. Cocksure, she must have seen those leaves spreading everywhere. "Help...please." again that ugly tree rustled. I got in a fix whether to go ahead or to give up, but repeated Beefy words compelled me to see there and that ugly dull tree started gleaming. Suddenly it turned into a crafty dull grayish enormous door. I scrutinized it. The door was really huge alike royal one. It had several tiny square sections, but the tiny thing borne by each section was not visible from far - off. What was it kind? I wondered what that was. Well, now nothing can stop me daring ahead, so I went on firmly. Anyhow, I wanted to figure out myself. Coming nearest to it, I found it was a swing-door having a pair of big iron ring on both the doors; perhaps used for knocking, I thought. And those tiny things were nothing but bells, which could not be, rang individually.

In spite of being engrossed, I felt someone hurried by my side. Well, as usual nobody was found there. Forget it; now my shivering legs got strength and finally, I resolved to get inside. I did not have to push the door; it was open by just touching it. Jingling of rusted bells with creaking of the door was enough to scare one, but I was not so feeble. I entered with a zest.

A dark gloomy but very spacious hall was a big surprise as I stepped in. I strongly felt to come out and confirm the outer structure of build up, whatever, as I could not believe a door- only door- single door, sorry! Double-door bears so much internal space. Well, this was irrelevant- off- course- my suspicion. Every door bear something, internally, isn't it? During my mental debate, I did not even realize that I was on the steps, upstairs. I could see it with the help of light, which beamed from the topmost broken roof.

Partly broken wooden stairs would not have let me to climb up, but somehow I managed and found myself in front of another scaring door. This time, I had to try my efforts to open I t "Chink… choonk…chink… choonk…" suddenly I heard this from the deep somewhere inside. I followed it, which was leading me towards right. I don't know why I was a bit of afraid to proceed, yet…

That long gloomy lobby led me towards the noise. It was unbearable noise of wooden swing, moving itself nobody sitting on it. I shrink back at once. I had thought to find something more venturous, and found rather dreadful. Suddenly, that swing stopped moving and it formed in several steps, again my legs started shivering, it was getting worse now. However, I thought of reckoning the steps, rather going on climbing randomly. I started one… as I climbed… two… three… four…five…six… seven… eight… no it was half… next there was nothing as I tried to step up. Only a beaming ray of sun helped me to see downstairs. What was there? Well, it did not look like any treasure-filled chest or a chiffonier. It looked an awful, terrible, and dangerous track like might lead me where? God knows.

It was wise to get away back, but curiously, I felt to step down. However, there was no way to get down, otherwise jump bravely. So I lifted my leg and …b…a…n…g…something kicked me, oh freak! I tumble down; and where? I was on the staircase? Oh No!

A loud uproar around me forced me to get up. I lie down on the stairs, beside the spectator's row. Many of them were still not able to control their mirth. Well, what was so much funny about? Who cares, I was not drowsy, no, not at all, but what had happened was not a nightmare. Moreover, these bleeding knees and elbows of mine can prove it.

To get the situation, I climbed down near the railing and almost ran the field, followed by the whole crowd. The net was torn off vertically and I got the whole course in my mind.

A torn net was that scaring door; hardly could I open it, passing a part of ground in the right as a lobby. Assuming the railing as that moving swing, for a while, I stopped there and found those steps to climb up. Nevertheless, those were the steps leading up to the top row. Therefore, I stood on the slender wall of the top row and was ready to jump almost 45 feet down straight away to…

It was that Veronica, who kicked the ball high which; bashed me and I rolled down the steps. Should I thank her to save my life or twit her on hindering me to unveil the clandestine?

Suddenly, I felt something heavy on me and I walked out to the changing room to the loud bombardment.

"Herbriea, what's wrong with you? Why you tore up the net? Has this been your practice? Have you faced anything weird truly like before, or it is your fear to lose the game?"

I stopped, "Well…" I said, but leave it and I walked in as early as possible. All the players, coach, teachers and few more, followed me. Next few minutes I came about many expected, queries, but to answer, any one of them may crop up many unwanted queries. So I just kept quiet, though it was awkward.

<u>Chap-5</u>
<u>Haunted</u> <u>Terrace</u>

Smash…smash…smash… a ball went on hitting the net, kicked by a broom. I enjoyed flying up in the air and when my team players brought the ball near me, I turn sideways and kick it with the bristles of the broom. "Hurrah!" we shouted, on our fourth goal. The viewers on the land were enjoying with us. We used to hop into clouds and twist around; this was an ineffable experience for me. While twisting again, I saw the ball coming nearer. I rushed to grab it, but suddenly I was smashed into. A sudden attack made me to lose my control and I was about to go down. Somehow I tried to balance with the broom, but again I was swirled with force. The anxiety took the place of excitement now. Before the lethal thing can come to and hit me again, I spin with the broom, bent down at the last moment and saved myself. I felt its razor sharpness very closely. I also happened to have a quick look and found it was a brown leaf with sharp veins that can cut anything. It wasn't alone, but followed by several leaves alike. Drops of sweat were dripping from my forehead now; the broomstick started slipping from my watery hands as I saw those leaves flying back towards me. I skip my beat and . . . ALAS! . . . T…R…I…N…G… BANG… I was dropped down the cot; light was switched on and my nightmare ended. I was panting for breath. While wiping my forehead, my fingers got red. I went to the washroom at once and saw my whole face having cuts and the blood was flooding out of them. The next moment, I stepped down to show my real wounds to my chums so that they could trust me fully.

A big surprise, the ground floor lobby was filled with pupils. They were mumbling beside the notice board, something important I guess. Mouzami and Nanisha too were present. They beckoned me, to this, all the others turned to see whom they were calling.

Seeing me, the mumbling stopped for a while; I know my facial wounds were going to hit the latest breaking news of the school. All the girls went aside to give me the way, obviously they were scared. Today I was an alien to them. I ignored this, and proceed.

My chums told me that the first semester examination was to fall within ten days i.e. from 1st October to 14th October. And the timetable for the same was mentioned in today's Notice. But above all, I was trying to find the sign of their worry for me, to feel their care for me that, I had always had for them, but nothing. Nanisha was blankly explaining the timetable and Mouzami looked more concerned about it.

It had never been so tough for me, but my behavior on the field shocked everyone. Football was my favorite game, though, very few girls managed to play this, I had always run down my rivals. However, the last match failed to behold the viewer's trust. Well, I was not defeated while playing, but by my mental disorder that came to the fore.

It was 22 September 48 hrs, Passed to football match. Today on Monday, I was called to analyze my stress and mental disorder test reports. Maybe even my chums believe that I am mentally ill and thus they least bother for me. They were ignoring me, my real wounds. However, I was not going to give up like this.

"Mouzami, Nanisha!" I said "Didn't you notice all these . . . my wounds the real ones." I showed them by touching my face. When I told them they examined my face with a surprise. Even few other girls noticed my wounds.

"Herbriea, there is nothing on your face, it is clean." Mouzami whispered without moving her lips.

"Don't trick me. I know, now you don't trust me." I was annoyed, "Look, look at them, even they can see," I pointed towards the girls nearby watching me. "And you... my best chums, how you can do this to me?" I said with a sheer disbelief.

"It isn't so. Look, come . . . come here" and they took me to the washroom.

I wasn't surprised but disappointed. I thought at least this time I would be able to prove myself. However, there, neither was any sign of wounds nor the blood marks. "Impossible, I had them. . . I swear... I just got them as I was out of the nightmare." Then I told them about my dream and how I got those wounds. Even they were surprised that where the cuts have disappeared. We came out usually discussing.

Our discussion paused as Veronica entered with her two hopeless friends and behind them was, Merletta. This showed that good and bad thing follow one another always.

Veronica was sure to take piss of me. She did not even have to strive to gather a mass beside her. This proved my Misfate.

"Hello friends" same old tricks, but it worked, as each of them noticed her.

"Somebody needs a great applaud here. Come on friends, put your hands together and clap for our GREAT CHAMP- MISS HERBRIELLA GOLD, FOOT OF GOD- MARADONA OF MINERVA, and BRAVO! HATS OFF! HERBRIELLA...TAN...TAN...TAN..." All those dunderheads followed her. She then came closer and sheered loudly, "HERE I PRESENT A BACKBONE ...oops! Sorry I guess you all won't agree right. Okay for you'll sake, Girls," and turning to me she said, "I hope you won't mind, Champ." "Okay friends on your behalf I would like to call her a BLACKSHEEP," except for few of my well-wishers, rest all chortled with her.

Although, the last match had cut me up terribly, besides, the Veronica's behavior made me more depressed.

She continued, "I guess, you can bear with me a few minutes more. So..." "ENOUGH IS ENOUGH, VERONICA" Mouzami could not resist, "There's no reason to blame her and anyway, you are not that person." Mouzami pulled up Veronica. Only she had the guts to stand against her wallop.   .

How Veronica could gulp this. She has to show her part. She turned around arrogantly and gawk everyone present nearby. I remembered her words threatening me, I felt embarrassment, and thought to pocket an insult, anyhow.

What and how she did, but to everyone's surprise, she plucked out a very beautiful flower bouquet and hand it over to me. All the students were puzzled and stupidly went on staring her and I stupidly touched it and again slipped into another world. *Where everything seemed familiar to me, I guess, I have been here before, same orchard, flowers, red carpet, same huge palace and now I was able to read those words. I read them aloud, "JHAALAAM DEVAA DADAATI MARGA." Oh! Can anyone tell me it's meaning? It sounds different unknown language that led me to my wit's end. Yet I tried to muse…*

"Helbliella" Oh! Gosh! Merletta not again. I mug up the words, ignoring her. "Herbriea! Stop dreaming." Mouzami said firmly and pulled me out of another world then. The lobby was empty now with Veronica. The students left for the breakfast except four of us. As usual, what I saw was vanished, but it left out the flower bouquet, that glittered yet.

"Did you see?" I asked my chums.

"What?" they asked the same old question.

"Oh come on now don't say you haven't seen the palace and those words i…i…just mused and…" I was panting.

"Herbriea, please calm down" Mouzami said and I got that yet they were unaware. Suddenly my eyes fell on the bouquet that has been left out. I picked it up, but Nanisha snatched it from me and threw out.

"There is no need to keep this," sanctioned Mouzami. I thought of explaining them that how much it was important to me, but Merletta was too young to ear this kind of stuff. Perhaps, it was not a good idea to convince my chums without any marks. Therefore, I joined them towards dining hall.

Merletta Bergner was from Zaire, South Africa, lost her parents in earthquake disaster. Her mother being an Indian, Merletta was shifted here, as her parents found it a safest place on the earth. She was the cutest, youngest friend of mine, always trying to be with me and even I enjoyed her company the most. Her big brown watery eyes drags me deep in her innocent beauty and her white transparent skin soft as wool, feels like touching all the time. This was her first year with us. I remember her first day when she had refused to have food and went on demanding for her parents. It became tough for all the teachers and wardens to calm her and tell the truth. To help junior students and new comers was one of my routine. I try to help them to adjust with new surroundings. So I tried to be friends with Merletta but she seemed stubborn. Yet for today my strong attachment with Merletta, I would thank Veronica. Yes, on the same day Merletta saw me being humiliated by Veronica and she came to know that even I was, orphan like her. She then stepped ahead towards me and since then an eternal relation tied us.

After finishing my breakfast, I stood in front of a Clinic's door. As I was going to turn the latch, "We cannot hide this from her." Dr. Teasel's voice was heard.

"But we can't even tell her, she is already disturbed," Mrs. Brook's voice. I wondered at her presence.

"Maybe, her mother's letter helps her out." Dr.Teasel said.

"Hope for the best." Mrs. Brook sighed.

When there seemed no discussion further, I knocked the door.

"Get in." said Dr.Teasel. As I entered, they pretended to be normal. She was sitting on the chair behind the table. She got up as I entered. She was in high collar off-white shirt and light brown trouser. The cuffs of her shirt were folded till her elbows, as usual.

"Had your breakfast," asked Mrs. Brook

"Yes, Ma'am" I replied. Mrs. Brook wasn't looking up today. I felt very awkward to face her after the football match. But she did not look concerned about it, only a bit from her face was missing. She was in polo neck jersey and parallel pants.

Dr. Teasel asked me to lie on the cot to the right. There were two cots opposite to each other and on the left one Mrs. Brook was sitting. A stool beside the cot helped me to get on it. Dr. Teasel immediately started with her testing. Her calmness was ought to be appreciated, in spite of their discussion just a while ago. Her deep-set eyes scanned me deeply through her oval eyeglasses. She was just like her eyes- deeply lost.

"Done your today's exercise" while moving a stethoscope on my chest she asked.

"No 'Ma'am'… I didn't feel like doing." I expressed. We were always advised to reveal whatever we feel physically and mentally in front of a doctor.

Dr. Teasel cleared her voice and turned towards Mrs. Brook.

They together stared, me; might they do not expected this.

"Okay, Herbriea, don't you worry you'll get through this, but for that you'll have to open your mind." Instead of Dr. Teasel, Mrs. Brook said this.

"CHIT EKAGRA that is Meditation is the best exercise for you and that we'll be doing now." Dr. Teasel said switching off the main light. She then sat beside me, placing her finger on my temple. She asked me to close my eyes.

"Herbriella, now stop thinking anything and take a deep breath…right…good…one more and now concentrate on your breathe alone." She ordered me. The room became Z dark, except a zero bulb over my cot was on and I could feel it through my closed eyes.

"HERBRIELLA YOU ARE FEELING SLEEPY… YOU ARE GOING

TO SLEEP… YOU WENT TO SLEEP… These words echoed in my mind and I was supposed to get asleep, but that yellow flash did not let me. *Instead, it led me to that awful track…a basement place in the door I had visited during football match. Today I need not have to jump; I was actually in. Rather we could say it a long dungeon…never-ending… horrible, too. I walked with my eyes moving both the sides but no one was there. I continued… a very little movement from my back, and I immediately turned around.*

Oh! Jesus, Oh God! A complete scope was covered with the thick roots instead of sidewalls. I moved my head upward and saw the roots grown on the ceiling also, the roots were thorny blazing at the tip like blade and then something moved beneath my legs…oops, the same thorny roots moved pitching me on every move. I lost my balance every time I tried to get up. It was not enough, the roots on the side wall started tearing apart one by one with the flow of red fluid… it was the blood. I realized that I was trapped … I tried to think on getting out… but… "Oh! Jesus… please help me… my mistake… Oh! God… give me power… please give me power…I want to live, God," the words flew out from me as the gaps went on widening… "I will never fight with Veronica, please Jesus, help me out"…but now the root one by one stretch out to grab me…I moved back I went on blabbering… the roots from my back too stretched out and even from the ceiling they lean down and the one beneath me rolled up on my legs and they together caught, me and suddenly I yelled and with this, the bright flash smack the roots all around and…I swiftly opened my eyes… thank Jesus…thank God Okay… Okay…chill babes…chill ye… no problem… I am yet alive. No rooty business beside…I felt sweltered… my throat got choked… sweat drenched me throughout. However, I was relieved to see Dr. Teasel wiping me with a towel.

"Calm down, Herbriea, it's all over. Don't get afraid, be free." Saying this Mrs. Brook handed me a glass of water. What will happen with only a glass? I drank three more in one sip. Yes, now it is okay. So this was the scene, I was not actually in Hell, it was my … Nightmare… or illusion…or something really happened… difficult to get.

"Fine, Herbriea, now tell me whatever you saw." Dr. Teasel said. Well, I was not worried to tell them, but my doubt was, would they believe me? Should I tell them or no? Or should I tell everything or only my today's …whatever… I was bamboozled.

"Don't worry, Herbriea, you can be open with us" said Dr. Teasel.

"We want to help you, trust us," Said Mrs. Brook soothingly. I got confused and I strongly missed my chums right now.

"Ma'am, not exactly but I saw many rats in our Dorm, and Ma'am when you threw that flash, all the rats ran away." I did not want them to guess anything weird, so I lied.

"When Herbriea?" Dr. Teasel said doubtingly. Well, then I wonder who sparked my life, or else within no seconds I had been chopped by those wild thorny roots. Not letting Dr. Teasel to read my mind, I stopped thinking.

"Well, Herbriea you said something in another language, do you remember?" asked Mrs. Brook.

"Uh…ah… ann…No…when Ma'am, I said nothing." I truly tried to recall but my words did not satisfy her, yet she kept, mum.

I found some confusion between both of them; they wishing to tell me something were hesitating on some point. I guessed, they doubted me to come around with them.

"You may leave, Herbriea." Said Mrs. Brook beckoning Dr. Teasel to keep quiet, "and…anyhow your other reports show normal state, so now you are okay to continue." Instead of me, they were more eager to get me out instantly.

"Okay Ma'am, Thank you Ma'am." Same desire here, as I was stepping out. . .

"Wait!" Mrs. Brook yelled from behind. "Wait a minute." Saying she went inside the other room and after a while she came out with something.

"Take this with you." She handed me that antique piece. It was the chest looked years old.

"Ma'am what's in this?"

"Ugh . . . well, your Mum's letters" she replied while glancing at Dr. Teasel.

The cool wind from the windows blew around me and I took the box closest to my heart.

"Oh! Its . . . it's very . . . much thank you Ma'am." I forgot the apt words to express.

"Well." Even she was able to say only this much, but her eyes were filled with the gleeful relief.

 "Yes Ma'am. Thank you." I said and almost hurried out.

[As soon as Herbriella left, Mrs. Brook again went inside the other room. She opened the drawer and took out an envelope which was already unsealed. She viewed the name written on it. It was addressed as 'To my sweet little daughter Herbriella Gold' from your Mum Ms. Kathy Gold. Mrs. Brook pondered for a while then put the envelope inside her handbag.]

As usual, my chums came to receive me.

"Did you tell her everything?" asked Mouzami.

"Oh Wow! What's this lovely thing?" Nanisha shouted and took the box at once. She was very fond of antiques as I was. They started studying it. It was a wooden box of dark reddish purple color having a petal shape. I had never seen such a weird shaped box unless it was an antique. The upper part was decorated with the cutwork copper design. Edges and corners were carved beautifully. Nanisha tried to open it but... "Not here." Mouzami stopped her. Anyway I was more interested in the stuff

it carried. We left the clinic area and headed towards our dorms.
Clinic was quite far from our Dormitory, I asked my chums to climb up
the school terrace that fall on the way, they agreed. It was an off day so
no one would be there to disturb us, not even school bells to ring
frequently. At the same time, the school must be locked! No matter, we
had the solutions. We knew the felon entrance; it was from the broken
glass window of the girl's common room on the ground floor. Its main
door latch was broken by Veronica's routine duel with somebody, so
then it was easy to get out of the room, unless the guard in charge does
not aim us.

Somehow, we got in and went upstairs. "But wait, is it wise to climb up,
being it a haunted place." Nanisha asked.

"Tut, rut! This is all nonsense." Mouzami snapped.

"No what I mean was, today being an off day and nobody to…" lisped
Nani,

"To what?" Mouzami cut short her, "Oh! I am cheesed off this canard."
Mouzami said on extreme.

 After attesting the guard's position, we all briskly climbed to terrace.
Nevertheless, Nanisha was moving her head in all directions to grab the
sight of something unexpected.

Same old place, we use to sit here during our break-time. As soon as we
took our old place, Nanisha tried hard to open the box, but she couldn't.
Not because she can't but because she was directly shot by Mouzami's
big eyes. She then gave it to me, and I opened it finally. As it got opened
a sweet aroma spread out and I tried to smell my Mum. The inner part
of the box was covered with golden green velvet. There were few
envelopes. I picked one envelope and took out the letter. Aroma sweeter
than before spread out. The paper didn't look as old as the chest was. I
unfold it and found many colors painted in the margin. Mum had known
my likings for colors, and she had always bought me loads of them.

"What's this?" Nanisha asked pointing towards the writing in it.

"It seems a kind of code language." Mouzami answered. The letter was in English language, only the alphabets were jumbled among one another.

"Yeah right, Mum taught me when I was a kid and didn't know its importance." I said. She had always preferred me to write her in code language. Well, the reason I could never guess, but I enjoyed it like a game.

"Doesn't matter Herbriea, you will sort it out." Nanisha said.

"Yes, she is right dude." And Mouzami patted me. I closed the box and kept in my lap.

"Well, Herbriea, will you tell us again about your experience?" asked Mouzami.

I craved for the chance and they gave me. I started from the procession day, then how I came across that silhouette thrice and in front of Palace twice and muse up those unknown words. I told them in detail, about my strange behavior, on the field during the match; this scared them. I was sure they would be horrified to know that I'd not only seen the dreadful dungeon, but also had been there without any armed precaution and had truly snatched my life from the jaws of doom. I told them about the language I spoke to get out from that dupe, which I guess was unknown to them too.

"What words did you spoke, Herbriea?" asked Mouzami.

"Err... it was something like 'aakar' no 'skar jewel' err... no I don't remember, I forgot."

"Did you tell them about this?" Mouzami asked.

"No, I remembered just now."

"Herbriea, you've memorize few words from your dream palace too, right?"

"Of course"

"Can you say?" Nani asked.

"Uh… well, not sure."

"I hope you can spell them." Mouzami was just sure.

"Yeah certainly." and I wrote those words on the floor with only fingers, Mouzami read them at once.

"Wait a sec, wait." Nanisha interrupted suddenly.

"I've seen these kinds of words somewhere." Saying this she tried to recall her memory. "Oh yes definitely, you'll have to ask Mrs. Chaturvedi about this." And she turned, pink.

"Have you gone insane? Why would she answer us?" Mouzami truly lost her control.

"Mouzami, I've seen these words in the books which Ma'am was tearing into pieces."

"What? Why? And how did you know?"

"When I had gone to help her in paper work I saw her tearing the pages from several books and burn them finally."

"Did you saw properly all the books were same with same words?" Mouzami asked with puckered brow as usual.

"Certainly, I did try a book to read but couldn't. First I thought those were Hindi books."

"Exactly, the words I mused seem to be Hindi language, but they sounds different, listen 'JALAM DEVAH DADHATI MARGHA' aren't they unusual?"

"Right Herbriea, but then to ask Mrs. Chaturvedi is alike to bell the cat." Mouzami was right again. Routinely, both of our eyes got fixed on Nanisha.

"What? I am definitely not that brave." Nanisha gave her explanation stealing our gaze.

"One more thing." I remembered later.

"What is that?" asked Nanisha ardently.

"Do you remember those brown leaves? … I saw that again… in my dream… today morning. They moved like strange creatures." I said pensively.

"Dreams are all about the stuff we face during our routine, so unreliable." Hard-nosed Mouzami said.

"But what about the wounds I got, I had never faced such stuff in routine." I penetrated deeply.

"Don't you think, your problem has increased after you had gone for the divine treatment?" asked Mouzami.

C…L…A…N…G… a sudden noise from outside the door disturbed us; we got up to see, what had been happening.

"Beware" warned Nanisha. We got her.

"Don't worry Nani, unless it is Thomas, or else we would be thrown out of the school." We knew the rules better.

"Let's leave," I suggested.

While stepping up we had closed the door, but now it was opened. We clench our fingers with one another's and stepped down.

Not to utter a word, it was understood and not to make the footfall noise. Nanisha, now walked between us, it was better, we didn't wish to take a chance. It was very dark except a zero bulb was on above the statue of Jesus Christ, on third floor.

Jesus' back touched the wall in the center and was facing the staircase. Therefore, when we go up or down the stairs, we were able to have Lord Jesus blessings. While we came on the first floor, we saw there was total darkness; again we clenched our fingers tight. Nanisha didn't allow us to get down, but we soon had to, so I pushed her. Yet, we dared and step down slowly. Definitely my chums too, might be regretting on our own faux pass, but no use, we had to proceed.

Somehow we came downright in front of the Lord Jesus, my chums kept moving with their head down but I was soon dumbfounded. Lord Jesus

 Finally, we reached near the ground floor but, we were on fire yet- Thomas.

"Hush! Now don't fluster, be careful, he must be somewhere around." Mouzami warned. She was more worried for the trouble to the fore and Nanisha was moving with her eyes and mouth wide open. I was thrilled and relieved to share this with my chums. Without wasting a moment, we got into the girls common room and closed the door at once.

"Thank God, he was in the washroom," revealed Mouzami.

"How did you know?" asked Nanisha, she was now able to move her eyes and mouth normally.

"Duffer, I always keep my mind open not just eyes and mouth like you. No one except him was going to use washroom on off day, got it?"

"Don't argue we are still in the midst of a river." I reminded them.

"But Herbriea, we are not in the river." Asked Nanisha and on this Mouzami was going to rail her but I beckoned her to keep quiet and just work on getting out of here. I confirmed the situation outside and gave them "All clear" signal to follow me. It was difficult to come out instead. However Jesus was with us. The clouds started sprinkling and we had to rush throughout the muddy path, but slowed down when we were near the dormitory.

"Are you sure, it was that same." Nanisha asked as we entered their room.

"Yeah, damn sure, it had worn same dress."

"Same?" I asked curiously.

"Why, didn't you notice? It was dressed in Indian clothes." Mouzami Replied.

"So what? And why do you call her like that? She was a girl." I was surprised on their talk.

"Yeah, but it was the girl's... spirit." Mouzami said proudly as if she was the first one to see that.

"Don't puzzle me, Mouzami; tell me if you know anything." I said desperately.

"Okay then listen, first don't ever discuss whatever we saw," she paused for a while like in stories.

"Secondly, it was really a spirit. Yes it was a spirit of Kesar- an eighth class student from Kutch." Saying this she once again checked the surrounding.

"It was a traditional day celebration in our school, when she came across an accident and she was found dead beside Jesus on first floor-how? - nobody knows till today." She finished in mute voice.

"But Mouzami, why is the terrace scope forbidden, when it actually happened on the first floor." I asked.

"Yes, you are right but it happened when Kesar was returning from the terrace. All say that something weird she saw upstairs, so swooped down to save herself, but that something chased her till first floor and then she was found dead beside Jesus Statue."

"Oh! How sad!" said Nanisha, even I felt so.

"And so from then onwards the terrace usage is forbidden by any of the ward." Mouzami Continued.

"One more thing" something stroked my mind … "though a year younger to me. How do you know all this? And why didn't you tell me when I found those keys?"

"I've heard Thomas telling this to Mrs. Rao, as he might have experienced it. And you know I don't believe just on ears, so I didn't tell you, I'd have been called stupid yet, I had kept you unaware." She said believing completely.

"When did it happen?" I asked.

"…maybe before 9-10 years,"

"That means she was of approx twenty three or twenty four, if she was alive today and might have left the hostel after completing her studies." I said investigating.

"What do you want to prove?" she asked.

"See you didn't get me, pretend we come by with any of her class mate then?" I tried to consider the left out.

"Then what?" they asked together.

"Then, then we can have nearly truth about Kesar's death." I said this from my sixth sense.

"Well, well, well… I guess we have other fish to fry." Announce Mouzami, but then she has to face Nanisha's interrogative stare. "Oh! I mean our exams are at the top on our list, list of deeds we aim to do, you see." She ends briskly avoiding Nani's stare.

"Oh! Yeah Herbriea, while preparing for our exams, we can also go through the books in the library and find about the unknown tongue that you spoke today." Nanisha Said.

"Well Nani, this isn't added in our list and anyhow nobody will allow us there, when we have all the stuff we need for our exams." Mouzami almost snarled at Nanisha.

"Chill dudes, don't get started again." I had to interfere. "I think you are right, Mouzami. We should be within." I got up saying this. Before stepping out, I turned back, and said, "But Mouzami, Nani's suggestion is also considerable, though it is chancy." They exchanged their look and I got their consent. I left for my room, thinking about Kesar, which showed a strong tie up with me.

<u>Chap-6</u>

<u>Hunt for the unknown Tongue</u>

The very first thing I prefer to do was to solve the code words in my Mum's letter when I enter my room. Drizzling day did not allow us to go out. So I wish to finish my work soon before the room gets crowded. Koyal and Fatima, two of my room-mates were busy in their work and rests of others were not present. Gently I kept the box on my cot, yet the four eyes were drawn towards it. I had hardly had any conversation with my room-mates, though we were in the same class, of course, Veronica being the cause. So they didn't react, just stared blankly. I jerked my head to forget their presence and began with my work.

 I opened the envelope again and took out the letter. The letter was of hardly a paragraph. I studied it and found the jumbled words that needed to arrange properly. It had been long time since I had not written this code language. This was going to be tough now. It was necessary to write down the pattern of this language first. So I took a page and pen and start on. I remember my Mum teaching me how to place the alphabets in this language. I visualize her writing the first half of the letters vertically on one side. I did the same. She then wrote the other half opposite to the previous letters. Again I followed her. That means the letter 'A' faces 'N' and 'B' faces 'O' and so on. Letters 'A- M' were to one side of the page and letters 'N- Z' to the other side facing them. Now the pattern is with me. Within seconds I understood that the letter 'A' is to be used in place of letter 'N' and likewise all the letters are to be used in place of the one they face. I started solving the jumbled words in the letter at once and rewrote it in the vacant space below. I read it as I finished writing. *"To my sweet little Doll, here I give you some of your own creations that you made when you were three and a half. For which you won the first prize in your school. I had never seen such real things created*

by a small kid. So I thought to preserve them in the special antique box as you are and will always remain special to me. With lots of love, Mummy."
And the letter ended. I opened the box again to find out my creations but nothing was there except few more envelopes. The things that my Mum had mentioned were missing. Above all, I didn't have a bit hint of another place if she might have kept there. My mind asked me to solve the other letters too but my heart said to go to freshen up for awhile. My heart is stuck with my friends. I found them and showed the solved letter. Even they asked me to solve the other letters but I am the one to get confused between my mind and heart and I know in this situation I need a break and something to concentrate again. Definitely to solve the unknown language was more important right now.

Due to lack of peace during daytime, I decided to do my mental exercises before going to sleep. I started with the light breathing exercise followed by other warm ups and then Meditation. Meditation means to throw out all the unwanted stuffs from our mind and make it empty for the better concentration power. That in turn helps us to stable our mind and prevent it from going vagrant.

Now, this was not the only intention of mine, I intended to avail myself with much more bizarre existence of which I have dreamt despite day light. So I choose this hour. Again and again my focus stopped at the unknown language that I spoke and yet didn't know its meaning. Dr.Teasel had asked me to set the time limit for practicing meditation from five minutes and then going on increasing until one hour, my capacity. This was the remedy prescribed by her for my mental disorder.

Suddenly, the darkness shoves out with the bright innumerable books all over. I have never seen such a dark and tedious place before. And...again a magic...one of the books went in the clutch of a girl...I knew this lass... I have seen her somewhere... definitely... very closely... Oh! No! She was Kesar... and ... she opened the book where Mrs. Brook's daughter Liz was in tears…slapping her leg lightly… but hold it…I saw something more… the leg she was holding, had a mark… it was like two tiny holes near the ankle…and drops of blood was dripping from it… same as it was seen on Kesar's forehead! Oh! It means… T…r…i…n…g… my fuddy-duddy alarm clock shocked me on my orders, not its fault.

The time was sharp 9.40 p.m. all my roommates were in the midst of their first round of nap. I did not wish to disturb them, so I had to help myself with a torch, a good ally of mine. I found my diary from the shelf beside my bed and without disturbing the dozing pals, I noted down all the facts that I saw during meditation. I also mentioned the first deed to be done early at the peep of the day. There was no time or chance to inform my chums, so I have to start alone.

It was not easy to get ready without any lights, but I didn't want my mates to wake up unnecessary. I took my belongings from the shelf and my eyes fell on the box. It was shining. The wooden box was turned into the transparent one. And I could see that it was the inner stuff that gleamed. Immediately I opened it and saw the number of tiny buds with bright colors. One by one they were blooming as the real flowers. As they stretched up, the aroma spread out gradually. I was blown to know that this was my creation. How did I do this? Was this really the one I had made? How is it possible that it did not show of when I looked for it in the box? Only my Mum can answer this or three and a half year old Herbriella who might have done this by a fluke or by…

The chirping of sparrows reminded me that I was getting late. After keeping the box safely in the shelf I secretly step out of my dormitory.

I thought to get inside the library before any studious get in, so I hurried towards it.

It was quite cool and dark out. The stormy cool breeze with the thought of being alone was shivering me entirely. I had to tackle it with crossing my arms. Once, I had thought of asking Mrs.Shakuntala, our Hindi teacher, about the unknown tongue but her tie-up with Veronica kicked that good thought out of my mind. Unnecessarily, she would get the chance to stretch the chewing gum.

Meanwhile, I reached half the way to the library, at quarter to seven a.m. Dark bushy dawn might turn bright any moment, so I rushed to finish the rest of the path, for nobody could find me going there.

Even the cleaners had to maintain their time allotted. Still seven minutes left to enter. Chatting outside the door, they didn't notice me chasing them. As soon as the big hand struck twelve followed by small hand at seven, two of them unlocked the library and rest two went upstairs to clean the laboratory. I resolved to get in just before they come out, until then I hid myself behind the giant doors opened outside.

"Aare, Shambhu, tune dekhi meri lughai?" While cleaning they again started chatting in Hindi.

"Kya, Rambhaiya, humko boolaya Nahin na." replied one called [Ram asked Shambhu that has he seen his wife. I had many Hindi plays on my tongue, so I did better understand them.] They continued.

I felt like time being stuck at one place, without waiting for them to finish I entered crawling down, I took left turn and went behind the counter table where Mr. Darcie-a librarian used to sit. I rubbed my fingers against the counter table and confirmed. Fortunately, they had finished cleaning this space, so no chance of them to turn up here unless something unexpected happens. I didn't wish to take the chance, so I hide in the space beneath the writing table.

Mr. Darcie was expected at sharp 8.00 a.m. until then I have 45 minutes, I counted… enough for my job or no. Well can't say. B…a…n…g I heard this for which I yearned to. The cleaners left the hall, locking it; obviously, Mr. Darcie had its key with him.

I started without wasting a minute. Flicking through the books of 2-3 shelves, I ceased for a while to remember what I was looking for. Oh!

Jesus closing my eyes I found that bold letters and got the aim. First thing was to look for the section regarding the subject I needed. Nowhere, all around, might be upstairs- an attic that was utilized fairly, staircase being inside the hall itself. Few minutes I will have to subtract. I walked long until the entrance and turned left to climb upstairs. Ah! 'Language' was the word written on the iron chip hung to divide different sections. My fingers went on flipping through the several books, but they were not filled with the stuff I needed. Strange! It was very important to find out the whereabouts of this unknown language as I have always come across it in precarious state.

However, I felt to check Mr. Darcie's Register book, Gosh! Again roll downstairs and subtract few more minutes, shoulders went down. With the heavy load, my legs moved towards the counter. Before stepping down, I checked the clocks position; big hand showed ten minutes to eight and warned me to hurry.

Better thought was to enter during reading hours and find out every nook and corner without any bare sword hanging up overhead. But Mr. Darcie was not even far away kith or kin to me to hand me his charge without any bombardment. I had planned to pick up the stuff and get out of here with the help of any of the ward when Mr. Darcie keeps him busy allotting books to readers. Now it seemed difficult.

I went through the register book of last six months, but I did not find any new or weird word in that. That means since last six months, no one has borrowed such kind of book. Or was it wise to search for it in library? Or it belongs to any other place or person? How could it be? I have clearly seen the dark place filled only with the books and books are obvious to be found in the library. But yes I haven't yet found that dark and tedious place. Where it could be? Stop, stop, and stop! Please, give me a break… it is too much. [This state may now add any pills to the remedy prescribed to me.]

Now what to do? Where to find? From where to start? Again, I felt my wit lurching me. K…u...n...Chq...K...U...N...Ch, k...l...u...n...k well, now time's up. Mr. Darcie unlocking the door was about to enter and no choice left for me than to find myself a safest hiding place. At this single moment I missed that invisible cloak worn by Harry, it might have helped me out. Well, I deeply wished and found the way in front of me. They say, when there is no choice left, follow whatever lies before you, I did the same, I followed the way lying before me. It led me through the long lobby packed out by the shelves of books both the sides. One would find her whole life short to go through these books; it took one complete minute to pass on.

I would have remained nearest to the front door, but the door I saw at the end of the lobby showed me hopes for another exit. Thank God, it was open.

Instead of full bright daylight, there were only two ventilators to let the sunrays pass through and make the dull, grey, or say ugly bookish room little bit of lively. Jesus! Instead of out, I got in. Entering in, there was shelf in the left, e…u… it smelled horrible. I lit up my torch, oh; it also carried few books. Although, I had to spend my time until someone comes to my rescue, I thought of going through these books. But it was chancy to move aside the broken glass sliding and besides, the main door could not be shut due to its broken latch, so go slow. Anyhow, I managed to take out those books- an 'Oxford dictionary'-first edition, "The game of life and how to play it"-Florence shovels shine- 1925 and few more books of almost half the century ago, this proved these books were replaced by its latest edition, so were kept aloof. My tiny lighthouse started dimming…and it went off… I had definitely found myself a fire bowl.

Cautiously, I reached until the main door and set my ears beside it to get the outer minutiae. No movement for next few seconds, finally I decided to go back, like a bad penny. As I pulled the door in, something fell down beside my legs and the dust spread out from it made me sneeze.

It was a dusty bundle tied with a sack rope, I felt by touching it. Slowly I closed the door that might bother Mr. Darcie, and then I went towards that part where, whatever light coming in can help me little. First I untied the bundle, followed by uncovering it from the dusty, dirty rag and then some 4-5 thick books got freed, but they need to be free fully, so fell down again from my tiny hands. I sat down to gather them, one by one touching it. But… wait… I touched one odd man; I took it out close to my eyes. It was not thick as others, it hardly had any pages inside, seemed. I kept other books aside carrying it under adequate light. The title of the book was 'History-2006'- unbelievable- why does the subject 'History" should lie alone in this store room like. I need to see inside. I removed the transparent strips of cello tape [now turned brown of dust] stick to all the open sides. One of my pets, Nail shaper helped me to open. As I predicted, it had no pages inside- not even the acknowledgement, in spite the outer cover was finely attached to the book's cover. Strange very strange, brooding over I flip the book- an empty book, without any pages- of any use-then why was yet looked after. ..   .. Perhaps, flipping helped and something came out from inside the edge of cover.[I told you so, never give up so easily, your efforts will never let you down- of course-at the cost of your patience and faith.]

E… u… it is still sultry! It wasn't so clear, but it felt like a very sticky part of any cloth, somewhere that was wet also. I wondered, the labeled name meant something else. Observing the label, it was found scratched at the left, down corner and the whitish yellow paper peeped out, as it was focused. Sorry, History, you need to be scratched fully. [Okay, so then I wonder why we were made playing the puzzle game, which included this 'scratching' activity also].

Within no time, the original subject flashed out, but to recognize it, I needed flash on it. A moment later, I was shocked and overjoyed to see that hooks and nut ball language. I came here looking for the same and luckily found it. 'SANSKRIT' was the word written boldly in English under the original title. Then I realized the place I have occupied now is the same one I had visualized during meditation. At least, my efforts paid me and I glimpsed my destination.

But my question bag never empties and now the question was that why this book had no pages and lied here weirdly? Why it was one and had no companion anywhere else? Why was it tried to hide?

"Aare, Pandu, dekho woh baksa storeroom mein rakh do." Mr. Darcie's voice quivered me.

"Sambhalke rakhana." Pandu- the cleaner was instructed by Mr. Darcie to keep any box of things in the storeroom, carefully.

I again got in a fix, Jesus; he might be coming here anytime. Full proof to catch me red-handed, oh God what to do? I badly needed Harry's invisible cloak right now. I heartily wished, I had learned some magic or had any magical thing or I haven't had come here or perhaps I wasn't a maniac. Oh, it's…DHAM! And I was dragged towards complete darkness. I was supposed to cry loud, but a palm across my mouth gave no chance, yet, the slow version came out. Oh! NO! It was GEORGE! I had a squint at him.

Thud! Pandu kept the box beside the broken shelf and Mr. Darcie followed him in.

Meanwhile, I was able to breathe and talk but this odd time, bound me to utter a word. Mr. Darcie and Pandu were finished off sorting the books from the box and turned towards the main door. We were on the right hand side of the door, but due to the lack of sufficient light, they could not see us. As soon as they came near the door, from where did God knows, a rodent passed away through my legs and I reluctantly, screamed out. Now nothing on the earth could stop Mr. Darcie to spot us and throw us out from the school itself. Oh! By swear I wished to be vanished or at least, something unexpected does happen that makes Mr. Darcie to leave this place, urgently or currently he feels short with his eye's vision-with any reason.

The foolishness of mine will definitely chuck my life out of the wheels. I joined my hands and begged, "O! Mighty powers, from the deep of my heart, I urge you to make us invisible...invisible... invisible...

[This made the remarkable amendment in the outer world; many types of giant foliage in various directions stretched and shake themselves. At the same moment, they threw a leafy fence around Herbriella and George. Nevertheless, due to its invisibility, they could not see nor feel and yet they were saved.]

"Strange, very strange," whispered George seeing Mr. Darcie's hand moving zigzag, at a distance, but not able to touch us. Mr. Darcie looked surprised and soon was tired of this game. So he quitted and left the room with Pandu. Just behind, George dragged me and without making noise, we followed him out in the hall. But the height of astound was when nobody from the wards present there, noticed our presence not even Mr. Darcie felt he was chased.

"At last!" I exclaimed running to the banyan tree behind the library.

"Miracle! Isn't it?" George expressed himself, "... Have any idea" he still could not believe what he saw.

"If I had any, I wouldn't have begged and anyhow ... how and when did you got there? And why?" I could not stop asking him.

"Wait, wait, first let me digest what I saw and then let me check my heartbeats." He said actually acting on it. After pausing for a while, he said, "the same thing I can ask you, but I won't as I don't believe in fairy tales." He got my back up.

"What do you mean by fairy tales and although, I don't need to convince you, okay?" ignoring him I started towards dormitory.

"Hey, Herbriella, I hope you have not left the thing you got there, take care." He reminded me. "So then, how about a cup of coffee" he asked lavishly and cooled me, as though it was no use splitting hairs with him. "Well, well, I guess it won't do." I said Pointing towards my wristwatch that showed we missed breakfast time and no time left to get ready for the school.

"Dash it, it is quite risky to be there, now, what to do?" everything unexpected happened and made me jumpy. I actually did not wish to miss the school and now I will have to be ready with my answers bag.

"Don Worry, Herbriea let's get vanished." George said, unknown to my condition.

"What do you mean? Is it so easy?" I lost my head.

"Why not, when you said 'invisible' thrice, it worked and then Mr. Darcie could not find us" he was enjoying like a game.

"Sh...Sh... Slow down, we've not left yet, and like when teacher repeat the word 'quite' thrice does it work always?" I said feebly, it was difficult to believe it happen because of me, though I wished.

"I have a suggestion." Oh God!

"What?" I asked carelessly.

"We should move towards Gate-2." He said secretly holding my hand.

"It would be rather more risky, you better know there's the bivouac beside and the candidates may spot us, no, no, we won't go there." I denied pulling my hand back.

"Yes, you are right, I know better than you. Those candidates have gone on furlough, so no one can spy us." He said as if he had been their relative.

"How do you know?" I asked.

"Oh! Herbriea can you behave normal... like a friend." He definitely got annoyed and before my behavior proves me abnormal I said, "Okay" permission granted and we proceed.

He took me from the bushes beside the Minerva Museum behind that lied Gate -2, but instead of turning left, he drove me towards right. After few minute walking, he stopped in front of a gigantic tree. "Wow!" I was impressed. Its trunk was so thick and spread wide that it can hide number of things behind it. He led me up on the branches and climbed like a gymnast, but I could not. "Climb up, Herbriea, you are good at it."

"Who told you?"

"I remember you were found on the topmost branch, that day" he thought I did it on purpose.

"Okay, but can you help me at least." I thought it wise to keep mum regarding. He reached to the V shaped branch, went through the gap and vanished.

"George, where are you? George, answer me, George…"

"Chill babe, chill" he said jestingly, leaning out from the space he had entered. Then raising his hand, he pulled me up and asked to hold the edge branch for support.

"Oh! My God, what a miracle!" that narrow gap went on expanding and formed a span with the help of entangled branches and leaves as a flooring and the walls and the roof, everything, everything made up of tree itself- a tree house- just like in Tarzan- cartoon film.

"Enough going crazy Herbs, now please get in soon before any alien grab us." I liked my new name. He helped me to get in and shut the tiny woody door behind me. Oh! How sweet! It was literally crafted out of wood.

"Now tell me why you came in that ugly bookish room? In addition, how? Moreover when?" I came to the point.

"One by one, why so haste? First I'll answer your last question." Taking a deep breath once he continued,

"I was chasing you when you reached near fountain, in the midst from where you hole up throughout the way, I saw you hiding behind the opened doors and then as soon as you crawled in, I chased you, but you turned left whereas I hid myself below the staircase." He stopped. I did not felt like commenting, moreover I was freed because of him.

"Now listen…" he continued, "I came there in search of question papers. Yesterday, late night I got the information that with the first beam of light, our semester exam question papers were expected in library." I was sadly surprised at his commitment.

"So, you chased me on purpose? Therefore, you did not turn up to…oh! My, my…then why did you joined me out? Why did not you stay there to take your papers? It had arrived… might be in that box, Pandu came to keep in." I was confounded.

"Oh! Genius! O! Superb! You are just fantastic, you are unique just like your name, HERBRIELLA and that's why you are famous." He praised me dramatically. "Nothing can remain hidden from you. See how easily you solved my problem." Now this was going beyond my limit, but he stopped boasting on my killer stare. I smelled something different as I cooled down. I knew George- the scholar does not need question papers before exams.

"Don't tell stories George, tell me the truth." I dealt with the problem directly and it proved an arrow shot into Bull's eye. George's cheekbones fell down along with his head. "Please George, I believe you my friend. Please let me know if you are concerned anywhere."

"Yes, you are right again, I have been watching you since the procession day." After great efforts, he let the cat out of his bag.

"Akka- you know her, that whimsical woman, who lost her voice-she, serves at my place. She told me so many weird facts that I could not stopped chasing you everywhere."

"You said she has lost her voice than how she tells you everything."

"Fortunately, she knows to write Marathi initials. She has even asked me to warn you."

"But why?"

"I don't know, but she said she had seen that thing, perhaps harm you."
He said so caringly.

"But why should anyone harm me? What have I have done?" that's true
I am a magic maniac, but I had never dreamt to harm anyone by any
means, rather I often come across the weird stuffs and get knotted.

"And she is also filled with the Liz's accident cause." I found those aloof
lines around me connecting with one another.

"I would like to see her George, now." I said impatiently.

"How come today, we can't" he frowned a little.

"No George, now no more wasting time, I quickly need to know
everything."

"Okay, okay, then shall we go on your magical broom?" he winked and I
beam.

"One more thing, how did you find this beautiful natural house?" I
asked while climbing down.

"I had made it, I love trees and everything connected to it. It makes me
cool." His eyes glittered while saying this.

"…then you and your friends enjoy being here."

"No, not my friends, nobody knows this, not even Veronica and Lial and
I expect you to hide this from your buddies also." He said possessively.
[Then why he reveals his secret on me, why?]

"Whenever I feel lonely I come here and chat with my friend."

"But now you said no friend of yours…" and he pointed towards the
thick trunk.

"Oh!" I found my dreams in his eyes.

"My friend- who gifted me this lovely house and want to know, Herbs,
how he talks to me?" I nodded.

"Okay…see" then he went near the trunk, gripped it tightly and said

"Hello! Bunny, how are you?" nothing happened until he repeated again…but then a storm of cool breeze slam into the leaves and they fall on George, just like a snowfall, as if to prove its presence.

"Wow! It's amazing" I got addicted.

"Hey, Bunny are you my friend?" he asked loudly and with this the branches on the outer sides leaned inside and flapped like a bird wings, every time touching George softly.

"Did you like my best friend- Herbriella?" Oh, I did not expect this much…from George. He looked excitedly ready for the response, but no signs.

"I think he didn't," I said sadly.

"No Herbs, otherwise he wouldn't have allowed you to climb up." "Once I invited Stephen here, but Bunny didn't allowed him to climb up, he instead badly injured him and made him to leave the place immediately, leaving his memory too." George laughed at his own joke, I too joined him and a sudden big storm of wind came along with the climbers entangled from all the sides and started showering flowers on me. It was amazing…incredible…ineffable… this miracle overjoyed me.

"Thanks, thank you very much, George" I felt short of words to express my feelings right now.

"Oh! It is amazing, Herbs, it's all because of you, I shall thank you instead. By swear I had never seen Bunny so much excited before." George looked ecstatic and his fair skin turned pink like girls, he looked awesome with his apt nose and a tiny brown spot on the right side of it. His light brown hairs showed his loyalty and made him more responsible. The cleft in the middle of his chin shimmer and his blue eyes watered as he went over the moon. [Well, I just tried to improve my visual ability.] For a while, we played with Bunny and enjoyed much more than any chaos game. It was all very natural, simple, out of the world. I was also happy to find a new friend of my relevance.

George Smith, not the only child of Mr. Jerald and Mrs. Amanda smith, lost his sister Christina, during earthquake disaster in Kutch, ten years back, when he was two years old. Just then, they moved in here.

Secret behind Kesar's death

"I think we must go back," George asked worriedly. We had been out for so long, say nearly six hours.

"But I think we have still two hours in hand." I meant to finish the work on hand, I was kind of a stick to person, do at a time.

"And then we can make any excuse." I was good at that also.

"But they will make out." He was right, those elders have enjoyed more Christmas than we had, with experience.

"Forget it; come what may, I'll face it." I pretend like a veteran.

"Wait George, what about your parents, they will come to know about your skip." I ought to worry for my best friend, now.

"Don Worry, my parents must be on their jobs. My father is a forest officer, he is in charge of 'Raan' forest up the hill and my Mum is a naturalist, so she accompanies him." While walking to his house he explained.

"So how did you get the permission to study here, whereas no natives are allowed in our school"? I asked.

"Mrs. Julianne Brook and my parents were neighbors in Kutch and together we had moved in here, on the same day. After coming here, her daughter Liz came across to an accident and she became lame." He became sad, I felt.

We reached near Mrs. Brook's place, I did not know they shared neighborhood here also. We entered the raw house beside our headmistress place. A maidservant opened the door.

Immediately George looked for Akka everywhere. "Kaay Pahije, Baba?" asked that thin, dark maidservant. "Akka Kuthe Aahe?" asked George in turn. We all were taught Marathi in school, so we knew it, though not thoroughly. She pointed towards the back portion of the bungalow. We rushed there.

Akka was busy with the gardening work. George went close to her and clapped loudly. This made Akka bounce on her feet. Seeing George she controlled herself and showed her teeth, but it did not remain wide open when she saw me. Suddenly, she seized both of us behind the wall of backyard. Asked George about my awareness regarding that, she warned him about. I wondered how she managed to talk the dumb language, but they say, "When a door is shut to you, turn around immediately to see the several doors open… just for you."

I told her or rather I explained my problems. Her eyes grew larger every time, as I went on narrating everything; even George was tensed. After I finished, Akka took us to her place- the servant quarter that was allotted her by George's parents. Not very spacious but a tidy place welcomed us. She took out some papers from the wrecked shelf-the only said to be furniture in her room. First, she checked the papers herself, but very soon got desperate. Asking her, she explained us, that, she had made one picture about that lethal thing with the only help of shadow she had seen; but now they were missing. She again verified and found the papers intact but the drawing on them was erased. How it is possible, papers were in mint condition. They looked fresh. I tried to ask, how that thing looked like. She said she haven't seen it clearly but as soon as she ran to rescue wailing Liz she saw the slithering shadow out of the window which left away the sticky substance stinking horrible that looked like a spit. And as she came back, the Liz's legs had lost their life. All this happened ten years back. That means this probably had the connection with Kesar's accident. I evoked something and took out that piece of cloth from my pocket. George beamed, on seeing this, even Akka's eyes; gleamed. She took it in her palm, kneaded, and smelled it several time. Yes, it was the same.

"What connection I have with this?" I asked her. First, she denied answering, but then she explained that I had been cursed. And the thing which harmed Kesar and Liz was not for them, but it actually had come to…and she stopped moving, even her eyes stopped moving and suddenly she inclined.

[A shadow up inside the George's house hides itself at once and watched them through the curtains as if looking over the movements further.]

We were definitely in Queer Street. Lakshami bai, that another maidservant assured us to look after her and we rushed to reach our dormitory before school gets over.

We were sure to be punished to play truant, but we decided to tell everything to Mrs. Brook. Anyhow, I needed to tell her about Liz before any further crisis. My heartbeats grew as we reached nearer. We ran, ran, and stood in front of the school's gate.

Thomas saw us and asked us the matter. I saw the watch, still half an hour remained. I was sweating like hell, so George put my excuse to the fore. We were asked to see Headmistress first.

[Herbriella and George were unaware of being espionage since library by an unknown shadow. It also followed them upstairs and as soon as they entered H.M.'s office, it hissed and flapped its tongue, swirled like turbine and gradually transformed itself into two little human bodies. Within a sec., those bodies took on ward's dress up to join the class and…

"Why so late?" asked Mr. Newman to two students just entered.

"We were helping Mrs. Chaturvedi in her paper work, sorry sir," said Veronica, though; Lial gave her a stupid look but she overcame smartly.]

Mrs. Brook, sat on the other side of the table, looked dissatisfied with us. "So why didn't you call anybody from staff, when you found her unconscious." She asked looking sharply towards George. [Personally, anger does not suit her.]

"And you, Herbriea, why don't you…" and she left the sentence with a deep sigh. I felt as if, I had cheated my Mum and how she would helplessly put down. I was sure to tell her everything, unless George had not forbidden me. "Okay, you may go to your classes." She checked in the clock hung on the wall behind us and asked us to leave. However, we were not punished but I felt guilty to disturb her mood. We left confused. My class was on the ground, for physical training, I too, joined them. Mr. Aiemas Newman, our P.T.Teacher asked me to see him after the class. Definitely, a detention, I started thinking for any better excuse. After few minutes, a peon approached Mr. Newman, and hand him a light-blue paper, sure, it was from H.M. Severe cold cuddled me and I started shivering.

Mr. Newman, took a break, went through it and then came near us. My ears rose up to be told.

"Here's a notice for all of you." He gathered us sadly. Oh no, it was a shock to find whole class being punished just because of me. I became eager to find the type of the notice.

"A picnic has been arranged…"

"Hurrah" without listening to him my mates roared and I breathe relief.

"Cool, first let me finish." And he continued,

"Your H.M. Mrs. Brook has arranged you a long tour in Diwali- [an Indian festival] vacation and she is taking all of you, means, the whole 5th to 9th class with her, isn't it cool?" and they roared again. Oh! So this was the matter and my thoughts just went out of track. How can I ever expect unkindness from Mrs. Brook- next to my Mum?

"Hang around, friends, know your picnic spot." No use, no work for my ears I was not interested to waste the time in outing.

"So, you are going for twenty days to Kutch, Bhuj." And I jumped on my feet. Oh! It is amazing, now I have lot of work.

Are not the happening leading me to repeat my thoughts, yes, definitely, I had a very strong tie up with all these. I rushed to discuss with my chums, but they had gone for their extra classes.

On the way down, I met Mrs. Chaturvedi and dithery I dared to ask her about 'SANSKRIT.' As if I have attempted a crime that my words made her eyes wide beyond the edges and then she examined me in suspicion. "Be attentive about your studies rather than roaming after unnecessary things." She yelled as usual and walked away leaving only disappointment for me. I sluggishly moved towards the steps. I remembered about my detention only when I came across Mr. Newman. He accompanied me to teachers' room and asked me the matter of my inattentiveness in class.

"Well, Sir it's nothing like that." I denied.

"Then why you wanted to know about the 'SANSKRIT." Mr. Newman's words charged me entirely. Hiding away the actual reason, I convinced him my necessity to know about the 'SANSKRIT'. He danced his eyes around the room, confirmed nobody's presence and asked me to see him at relevant time if I really need to know about it but without anyone's sense, not even my best friends. I promised him honestly and we departed.

[Mr. Newman asked Herbriella not to disclose her secrets to her friends… but what about her foe- Veronica got every minutia about their plans and snakes slithered in her eyes.]

Again, I came around the H.M.'s office and I heard Dr. Teasel's voice. I scratched my ears and… "Julianne, have you consider the risk over there." She sounded worried.

"I know Rose, but I had to, I need to dig up everything. Kesar, Liz…Gopi and now this…Herbriella… poor girl, Why?" Mrs. Brook was more worried.

"But are you sure she…" Dr. Teasel was cut short,

"Haven't you read her mother 'Kathy's' letter, something's connected over there." Her confident reply shot my mind. That means Mrs. Brook still have one of my Mum letters and that is more crucial. I strongly felt of acquiring the letter instantly… and the telephone inside buzzed. Mrs. Brook answered briskly and I moved. "WHO… AKKA… WHEN…oh no…" -these bold words stuck me there again. "Okay, watch her I'll be soon there." she assured someone on the phone. I was sure to tell her, but George pulled me back and took me downstairs.

"Are you crazy? You will definitely find us a trouble." He said, obviously, he did not know whatever I knew.

"What about Liz? She ought to know this." I told him everything.

"But Herbriea, this is not the right time." George again reminded me.

"Hey, dude, no class today?" Lial patted George and squinted at me. With a hope, he must not have heard us; I exchanged a worried look with George. George joined him out or says Lial drag him; I too had to move towards my dorm.

That night I passed in dilemma, until late I waited for my chums to turn up, but the class 4 students were made to sit long to finish their remaining syllabus. I was full until neck and needed to be empty, but I could not expect even George, at this hour. Again, my stuff- sweltering cloth, Akka, Mrs. Brook and Dr. Teasel's conversation, Kesar, Liz, Gopi, messed me up… Gopi? Who is this new one? However, above all my Mum's letter that can guide me, I know. Lastly, I cannot forget- I have to get ready for my exams arriving after two days only. I regularly watched the flowers in the box blooming with the sunrise and shrinking at the sunset. I was unable to believe them as my creation.

The next two days passed in preparing for the exams. And yet I did not forget to see Mr. Newman. He arranged in the school's storeroom where the game's equipments were kept and no one during the exam period was expected. So I started my sessions whenever possible.

The sun rose responsibly, the wind also blew studiously and helped the Minerva boarding's students to concentrate better. Seeing my chums busy schedule, I did not wished to disturb them with my problems. Even

I was required to be serious at least for few days.

During these fifteen days, several times, we came across and every time I controlled myself, on George's moral support. Yes, he knew my problem; he did not leave me and heard me patiently. His company made me stronger even against Veronica's infancy rivalry. Above all, I tried my best not to make him aware of my extra classes as I had been told.

Nothing weird happened during these days and I wished not. Moreover, I was relieved, on Akka's well being, she was better now but she left George's household work. One by one, we went on attempting all the papers. And the day came of which each student awaited- our last paper- History.

Before going to school, I went to see Mouzami and Nanisha in their room. They had just left for breakfast. I wanted to tell them about today's party celebration that George and I had decided to arrange and they were expected to help us. Feeling sad, as I was pondering, I did not realize when I opened Mouzami's History textbook lying on the floor beside. Why, I went on turning the pages and took out a leather strap leaning out which was not alone, it was tied with that rectangle shaped identity card, yes, it was Merletta's. Oh! No that silly girl must have forgotten here, then without this how she will sit for the exam. I must hurry up to give her. Nevertheless, one thing I got the hang of- How Merletta's card got space between the pages of Mouzami's book. How did it enter even into this room? Upon all this, I rushed to Merletta's room on first floor, I was late again; she had left, a minute ago. Might I will be late again so I asked Saloni- Merletta's roommate to give the card to her.

"She had already tied in her neck." Saloni said sweetly.

"But then what to do?" I murmured.

"Leave it in her drawer." She suggested it was a good idea. Opening her drawer, I found replica of my personal diary, (so, we bring up same hobbies) I took it out and found my two scalene stones beneath it. Well, well, now nothing to say or to think. I just kept everything in my pocket and ran to attempt my last exam.

I wrote hurriedly all the answers, though, I had studied thoroughly; I was not sure for my accuracy, this time. Without caring to recheck, I submitted my answer paper and came out of the classroom. I moved wildly all over the floors, maybe the material my pocket possessed made me so. Crossing away few classes, I came in front of the fourth class, but neither Mouzami nor Nanisha was found in between the group of students coming out.

I left towards my dorm, maybe I find them over there. Coming out of the school premises, I received a leaflet instructing us about the long tour to Kutch. I kept it in my pocket when George joined me and we both looked for my chums finely. They were found nowhere, none of their classmates nor did roommates know where they were.

The only way was to ask our dorm's guard in charge. He checked the register book and found that both have gone with their parents out of the scope and will be returning until next morning. "They can't do this to me." I was shocked to hear this, "I know their parents very well and they too, and instead they treat me as their own daughter only, George! Then…then why they didn't told me." Not believing their behavior, I asked George.

"You're right; at least they would have informed you." He said.

"Hi Herbriella!" Suzy said. She was my chum's roommate and I remembered something, "Suzy, wait, do you know where…"

She cut short me, "Oh! Yes, they asked me to inform you and I forgot, I am so sorry. They had gone with their parents and just…"

"Why? They needn't have to tell me?" I was surely annoyed.

"But they came to know just today morning before going to school."

Suzy said little guiltily.

"Don't worry; they will be back by tomorrow morning." She consoled me.

"Oh yeah, and by noon we might set off to Kutch." George said and I saw him idiotically.

"Yes, haven't you read the brochure yet? It's all written in that." I took out the paper and Suzy left us. The paper had the full details about the timings, no. of train, etc and even the list of accessories, which we had to take with us.

"George?" I was not able to think in the absence of my chums and recognize the weight of our true friendship. George too proved his weight to know everything whatever I found but girls' dorm was not the right place and finding no other place safe we decided to go to his bungalow. Well, again it was a cheating, we knew but I needed to unearth everything. We came near Gate no- 2, verified around if anyone following us and found the bivouac full of soldiers practicing their training lessons. We curved down and passed along the sidewall.

"Ugh…" being in this position for long made me uncomfortable. Within few steps ahead, I stretched up back. "Oh Now it's better, I am able to walk properly!" George held my hand and we waded the bushy way. With the rustling of leaves both the sides, I heard something more. "Hold on" I … stopped George moving and tried to listen better in that direction… no result. Going further again, I heard but the same result. How George looked into my eyes and then why we moved very slowly, I do not know, but it worked. As soon as we heard that third time, we turned back instantly and found one young but pale and sick boy wrapped in an old blanket. He looked confused maybe on our sudden movement. Being much older than we were he pretended to be fearless, but he was not.

"Who are you?" George asked him and without any more efforts, he opened his heart. He was Gopi, one more victim on the day when Kesar died.

"What was it? You saw?" I asked him.

He looked around and said in hushed voice, "No, I could only see the bit of black checked blanket that smelled horrible" His description matched with Akka's.

"What happened exactly that Kesar died and don't mind, but you are still…" I asked cautiously.

"Will you tell us in detail?" asked George.

He gave us a painful look and continued. "It was a traditional day and celebration was going on in the dance hall. Kesar and I were dressed in Kutchi traditional dress and were enjoying with others. Finding shortage of beverages', Mrs. Deepika asked us to tell Collin- the peon to bring the extra boxes from storage. We looked for Collin all around the dance hall, not finding him we went towards school." Saying this, Gopi looked around to be comfortable, maybe and sat on the pavement beside. In spite of sweaty climate he did not allowed that thick, itchy blanket even to be flap from any of its corner.

"It was dark and felt scary to get there. Though Kesar warned me I was stupid to take her there." And he sobbed. "Collin was busy repairing the fuse in candle light when we gave him Mrs. Deepika's message. He asked us to watch his place until he comes back. After he left with the box, it was that big noise to attract us towards the staircase and we randomly climbed up. We did not think at least once that… that it might be dangerous and it truly led us to the grave," he covered his face with his palms. "Oh, that horrible smell, still it stinks. We reached till terrace and saw the door was half opened." He freed his face from the clasp and I saw water was ready to drip from his eyes. "Oh! Again I did a mistake…" he started crying, finally.

"Calm down Gopi, it was not your fault; anybody could have done the same." George consoled him.

"Strong bad smell entered my head, when I opened the door. Suddenly from where some sticky substance sprinkled on me, I screamed and got back without bothering for Kesar and realized only at the down stair. Kesar did not follow me; I again climbed up slowly and found her on second floor steps with her eyes wide open. I called her several times but she stood like a statue. Finally, with someone's deadly roar and drenched with its sticky spit, she collapse down on the steps and I ran to my last breath." He paused to breath. "I then narrated everything to Mrs. Deepika. She and few more teachers rushed in a hope to save Kesar, but they found her dead beside Jesus statue on the first floor." "It was my mistake, definitely and I am paying for it." He said wailing like a woman. "No, Gopi, you have taken too much to your heart. If it was your fault then that creature must have harmed you also." I said those big people words.

"O! God, I shouldn't have been so selfish, and then this wouldn't have happened." Saying this he unwrapped himself and we saw hundreds of tiny boils that Gopi's body possessed. Only his neck to head part remained unaffected. George and me clenched our hands together and moved aside. He was in one-piece cloth covering his waist to knee part and he again hid it under the veil.

"It caught my legs first, and then went on spreading. My family had tried many doctors and even enchanters for eight years, but no results." He said but we were busy keeping ourselves aloof from him.

"Then what happened to your family." I asked, as I knew that accident took place before ten years.

"Don Worry, it's not infectious." He caught our hesitation. "Since last two years I left my family. I cannot stay long at one place, so I have to wander. Few days back, when I saw you with that piece of cloth, I could not resist, and came to warn you. And for this I think, I am alive."

Nobody talked for a while. "Water... give me water… ugh…" suddenly he became wild and threw away his veil aside. Luckily, George had carried his school bag to home. He gave him, he drank, he went on crying and we saw those boils gradually taking up his neck portion. "One thing is sure- my death. Two years back the last enchanter to whom my family approached said, I had been not only spitted but badly cursed by a dangerous evil, which was rather impossible to break or even cut down." His worst condition made us dumb. We watched him peter out into the wood until long.

<u>Chap-8</u>

<u>Bhattji</u>

Now of one thing I was relieved that Kesar and Gopi's matter was cleared and somewhat Liz's. Today's night was not less than yesterday's; I was yet full and had no one nearby. Anyhow, a fresh dawn follows after every bleak dusk, the bright shining moon in the dark sky reflected my belief, I asked for a wish to see my chums very first in the morning and went to bed.

My heart filled with hopes awoke me half-n-hour sooner than ever. Most of my roommates were snoring yet. I rushed to see my friends might have arrived but they had not. With a heavy heart and eyes, I started my packing. I gathered everything according to the list and those things also, which did not show up in the list.

Sharp at 9.00 am, after finishing the breakfast, our Headmistress called all the secondary students in school premises. George found me, Veronica too, so he did not utter a word.

"Okay, wards pay attention." Mrs. Sailee bellowed. All the students looked excited. "Good morning children." Headmistress Mrs. Brook held a mike. "Like every year, this year as well you are going to a long tour which would be learning with fun camp. Kutch, which lies in north-west part of India, is your learning spot this time."

"Damn, what we could learn there?" Soham from ninth class could not stop commenting.

"You restless, Can't you wait?" even Mr. Bellwright- an E.V.S. teacher, cannot wait of scolding him.

Unknown to the gossip going on far beside, Mrs. Brook continued, "You are going to study about the Earthquake disaster that took place there in the year 2000. Its post effects, Man's life after its occurrence, precaution taken to avoid it and lot more, personally. For this, you will visit many

93

victim districts that will again help you in your assignment." Saying this she peek all the students once and said, "So need me to quench you more?" she asked and Soham did open his mouth but before he could say something, Lara, a seventh class girl asked, "Why do we need to go to Mumbai, Ma'am?"

"As there are no direct routes to Kutch from here," Umang- an eight-class boy, instantly answered her question.

"Okay, friends you are expected to maintain the rules and don't forget to take your belongings along. Next, we will meet near the Bus. So be preparing." The clamor started after Mrs. Brook left.

Veronica got hold of George, this time and the group of students gathered around us. "So buddy, drifting a lot nowadays?" she asked him threatening.

"Look veronica, I don't want any issue, I can explain you." George was not a fire-eater.

"Oh! Yeah so, you are going to explain me- to Veronica. Okay than tell me how... how can you think even?" peppery veronica did not wished, but she stopped on Mr. Newman's arrival, he did not knew the recent scene.

"So friends, planning for new tricks?" He asked patting Lial on his back and we just smiled. "Okay, okay, don't reveal now, but don't try me. I am with you." He winked and we all laughed.

George went with veronica and I went to my dorm movingly- alone. I entered my room and saw my chums sitting on my bed.

"Where were you? Why you left me alone? I have to tell you so much." I was not able to control myself.

"Sorry, Herbriea, we're extremely sorry, but we were helpless, our parents came to take us and we have to go with them."

"But then what about me, I need you." I felt unsecured.

"Herbriea, as though it was no use staying here without you." Said

Mouzami and I remembered that the primary section was not accompanying us. Without wasting a minute, I started emptying myself from the library event until the day. Mouzami got me clearly but Nanisha required detail explanation.

"Don't worry Herbriea, now you have the right person with you and for that we are happy." Saying this Mouzami turned her face from me.

"You are not," I said bluntly. On this, she turned and hugged me, Nanisha too and we seize ourselves tightly.

"Don't worry, Herbriea you will find us whenever you'll need us, it's my word." "And we mean it." They both assured.

"But you will have to call our names thrice, okay?" said Nanisha and we cheered up as usual. I wished to see off them, but I had no much time.

After they left, I snatched out the thought of being left alone and started with the packing. I tried to adjust my antique box in the suitcase but it could not. Leaving it aside I packed rest of the things first and tried it again. Suddenly, there was a loud bang on the door and it did not stop until I opened it. It was George.

"Hey, did you see them, my friends?" I asked him.

"No, I didn't." he replied as if he had not at all seen anyone since long. He looked like doubting me.

"Herbriea, I am here to give Mrs. Brook's message for you. She… she… wants to see you right now." He said the last words briskly.

"You know the reason, tell me." Being constantly with him for so many days, I was able to discern him better. He reacted with tapering his eyes.

"You tell me, how your friends can come here, when Mrs. Brook received their parent's message stating that they have left directly from the Motel where they stayed yesterday."

"What? I don't believe." I was definitely shocked. "Just now they went from here and they had even assured to be with me … always."

"Un... maybe… that must be your illusion."

"No George, trust me I literally talked with them, touched them, in fact we hugged each other."

"Then how did Mrs. Brook got this message? Has she mistaken or she said on purpose."

"No George, I believe her and she can't be wrong."

"So it's all about the thing that's chasing you. Herbs, we need to find out." George looked deeply worried.

"Not just this, there's much more lying to be unwrap; but how?" I said pensively… "I need to go to Akka." I said decisively.

"But she can't even speak." George got impatient.

"Yes, but she knows to write, isn't it?"

"Herbs, we can't spare time at once. Only few hours are left for us to leave and we don't know her place." He was right.

"I have to find out George, I have to take risk now or never." I said earnestly.

There were mishmash looks on George, his frowning face turned to suspicion and then his eyes grew wide with a decision.

"Okaay, I am with you." He sounded modest rather than dramatic as usual. And those simple words were enough for me to count on, but…

"No, I can't risk you for my interest."

"So this is how you trust your friends."

"George, lot of weird things are happening around and it's all about me, alone."

"If it is about you then we are equally concerned. Even you cannot avert me to accompany you." He was damn firm and I could not refuse him. George had already packed his luggage, I packed my bag in muddle and we both rushed to see Akka. We did not wished to register our exit, so we went out through our secret way, as usual. Once Akka has told George about her village but he did not know her house. It took exact forty minutes to climb down to Dhapoli- a village where Akka lives. In addition, it took few more minutes to sort out her house from the row of similar houses build nearby near. It was typical a hut type as we have seen in our Geography textbook.

When we pushed in a bamboo door, we saw Akka lied in her sack bed, but not looked asleep. With a little hum, she changed her side and got up quickly on seeing us. "Akka, how did you come to know about my curse?" I asked her at once. I found positive response in her eyes, she got up to take a paper and wrote something in that. She wrote in Marathi language. Reading that, George and I, hurried out. Akka had mentioned the name and address of that Enchanter, who predicted about me and she stated it the only way to cut down the curse.

We reached near Junnar Lake where that Bhattji lived. George use to check the time regularly, so we may not get late. Now an hour left for our departure.

Bhattji, short and thin on top, did not look pleased to see us. Then to Akka's letter, he took us in his place, but not inside his math - that is a room for worship. After listening to us, he spelled on his fist for a moment; then he took out a black long thread from his fist. "This 'Taveez' will help you; tie it on her upper arm." He said giving the thread to George. George helped me to tie the thread, but immediately he left it as the thread started burning itself. This gave shock to Bhattji and his eyes remained wider. To our surprise, that thread did not leave its ashes as well, though it had burned completely. Bhattji asked us to leave instantly.

"But what about my curse, I cannot live with that all over." I asked him, as he was the only last hope.

"Sorry, it's beyond my control. The one who has enchanted you is much stronger than me and he will do anything to harm you. Sorry I am extremely sorry for that." He said everything in fear. I felt helpless; I saw my hopes dying and I cried.

"Can't you even tell us that why she is enchanted?" George asked taking my pain on himself.

"No, I can't." Bhattji replied in terror.

"There must be some another way, please tell us." George begged him.

"I don't know that; I have not that many powers," and something evoking he said, "However, I can send you to my Guru; might he can do something." Oh! At least, I saw few bright rays.

"He is in Gujarat at present and might stay there until month's end. See if you can reach in time, than it's your Luck otherwise…" George noted down Guruji's proper address.

"One thing I can do if you wish, wait." Saying this he again spelled on his fist and took out the similar 'Taveez'. "You are the nearest to her so can be his next dupe. And this will be your armor." He tied that thread on George's upper arm and waited to see the result. With the touch of it, I saw an inferno passed around George. "Did you see that?" I asked but they did not. "One thing you bear in your mind; never take out this, though in any emergency." We assured him and left. Only fifteen minutes left for our Bus to take off. We were damn sure to miss it. Yet we tried and found a help from one native, who was driving towards our hostel.

As we crossed the half of the way, our mail-van stopped moving further and we had to get down. Now unless our H.M. waits for us, we will surely pass up our bus. Due to some engines problem, the van stopped and needed a professional help. Fifteen minutes to climb up, no other way we saw, so we decide to walk all the way.

"George, I am sorry." I said.

"What for?" he knew for what.

"It's all because…" I tried to explain but he cut short me.

"No Herbriea, a friend in need is … you know better." I found full support in his shining eyes and my eyes shone bright with his trust on me. That was weird, during this hour, yet cool.

Chap-9

A voyage to Mumbai

We missed our bus. When we reached hostel, nobody was aware of our absence. Instead, they looked worried for someone else. We checked in our room to get our luggage but it was missing. I checked thoroughly under the bed, beside the shelf and everywhere but it was disappeared. I checked even the box was not there. Except of few care takers and the tenth class students the whole hostel left on tour. Frustrated we came out.

"Oh no, I told you so." Suddenly George became furious.

"Even I told you to leave." I reminded him.

"That's not the way…"

"Then to I asked you to quit."

"Oh… Herbriea you are just impossible." He was surely annoyed.

"I didn't ask you to follow me."

"Yes definitely it was my mistake." He again evoked me.

"So you admit…ugh." I had never thought he would say this. I remembered how he compelled me to take him along, so definitely I did not expect him to be rude. Unknowingly we came towards the Gate-2 where few candidates were yet exercising.

"Hey, George you didn't go for a picnic?" asked Bhasker who was one of the best friends of George.

"Well, we'll join them later." He said viewing me from his eyes corner, my eyes encountered with him and we chuckled together. By the time, we had crossed the Gate-2 towards his house. The hot wind squeezing between us chilled down cooling us thoroughly.

"Herbs, now it's better to be off from here." George said.

"Yes, but how they head off without us? Why they didn't noticed that we were missing." Finally, I burst out.

"They must have confounded."

"But they ought to be accurate."

"Yeah, and even my parents did not noticed." He said thinking something.

We went to George's house to sort out the situation. His mother was on phone talking about George's trip to somebody. She also showed her relief that she reached correctly at the time of departure otherwise, she would have missed saying goodbye to George and his new friend Herbriella.

"Oh! No this is unbelievable, I'm here Mum…," said George impatiently. Mrs. Smith stopped talking on phone and was surprised to see us.

"George… oh my boy… what's the matter? Why you are back?" she said in sheer disbelief.

"Mum…err… we had gone to…" before George could complete his words I interrupted, "Yes…err… just we reached the midway, Aunt and he remembered he has forgotten to take along…" and gesture him to handle further.

"Yes…err…Mum I forgot to…," saying this he rolled up his eyes around and "some bucks… my piggy box… I…I think I should take them." He did it, yes.

"Why not sweetie, you should definitely take em… in fact some more, you'll need them." Saying this she took out some bucks from her purse and gave it to George, caringly. Her round face wrinkled as if pouring out all the good wishes over her son, but became nervous as her son hugged her. She counted me only when I asked George to hurry up.

"Oh! how stupid of me, I didn't welcome you." Instead of feeling sorry for that, I saw an unknown fear in her small lifeless eyes.
"Never mind Aunty, we are already late."

"Sweetie, shall we go now?" I muttered in George's ears. He got pink and then red towards me, yet he looked sweet and I thought this was the right nickname for him.

"George, if she had really seen us off. Just think, if we were not present there, then who those two nuts akin to us were." I told him while getting out from his house.

"You're right again Herbriella, there is lot more to be unwrapped and that we can do only by following them to Mumbai and without their sentient." He said resolving.

"Well, you are free to choose."

"I know" saying this he leaded me ahead.

But how? This bothered both of us. We had never traveled to distant alone. So now, how to go there was a question. Through any private vehicle, yes it was a good idea. Then with whose help, that was another question. "Akka!" we remembered and rushed towards her, but going few steps ahead, we stopped as well, as we saw her coming to us. This was again something weird… unbelievable. Before she could ask, we explained her everything and she heard patiently.

"Pan, atta tumi kasha jaanar, baba?" she shocked us saying this. We were now able to understand her dumb language so we didn't expect her to speak like us. Anyhow it was good to hear her normally.

"Akka, Tumhi bolu Shakta?" asked George about her voice. She looked puzzle, we waited, but she did not reply.

"Ek vaat suchvu tumhala, patel ka?" she asked us whether we are ready to follow the way that she will show us. Necessity is the mother of invention; we would have accepted anything at this hour. She led us at the bank of Junnar Lake and asked us to remain there. I scruple to follow any unknown path; however, our reaching Mumbai was more important than this word 'How'.

"You said she won't be able to speak now, never, George?" I grabbed the chance and asked him.

"So I am astounded, too," "Anyhow, reaching Mumbai is more

important right now." He read aloud my mind.

After a span of time, Akka returned with a tall, dark giant looking man, he was rather creepy. I wondered the way he would take us through, on his beefy shoulders or what?

He whistled covertly, it happened that the vast craft, though wrecked, stood in front of us in the lake. Akka asked us to board in. That beefy giant was called Kalu and he will accompany us for our security.

We started our voyage with the nerves of excitement. At the last minute, I remembered something, so I ran forward towards Akka, but she was off from our scrutiny.

"George, has she mistaken?" I asked him when he was still waving towards Akka. I awed for his eyesight.

"Oh, common now think how this only small lake can take us to the vast bank of Mumbai, just think George, and just think and…" Kalu the giant stood behind him stopped me to say anything further. Seeing my gestures, even George got horrified and turned back.

"Hmm…hmm…" Kalu just drone and showed his teeth, he looked more horrible in that way.

The ship was not only broken from outside but from inside as well. Suddenly the climate changed with heavy pour and stormy hailstones. We ought to save ourselves, so we climbed downstairs into total darkness. Those wrecked steps led us down in the lobby, dark lobby. Only the light from the thunder outside helped to glimpse the inland. With the help of that one blue ray, I saw those teeny-weeny eyes at the end of the lobby. I pressed George's hand that I held. He got me but we did not dare to move ahead. We stepped up again and found one more lobby, darker than before. We remained on the steps for a while. Habitually, I looked for those eyes to come about again, when George asked me to climb upstairs. Sometimes the wish begged unknowingly from the heart is always granted, not only on the second but also on all the lobbies' end that we climbed up, I saw those eyes. We went on climbing, until we were deadly tired and the number of lobbies went on increasing instead. It was strange to find so many floors on this old, shattered ship. First when we saw this ship, it looked in ruins and was expected hardly any space inside, but it was a miracle to have several similar floors, though all wrecked and dark. Finally, we resolved to walk away the lobby.

As soon as we stepped on the flooring, the roar of thunderclaps filled our ears. I confirmed the time; it was 2.30.p.m. or a.m. as the sky was darkest than ever, as it used to be in midnight. Dreadfully, we moved further with the help of the wall beside. The first thing that came in my hand was the latch that without giving it the movement, the door behind opened itself. Only the darkness was sighted. Under the rumbling of thunder, we swayed with the ship and moved changing the sides consecutively.

"George, there are too many rooms I think." I said in a hush voice, finding similar latches and doors every time touching the wall.

"Yes Herbs, I am confused whether to step in or to remain out."

[Their decision may put them in trouble if they entered any of those rooms, as they were unaware of the evil waiting inside to munch them.]

"So let us toss, if Heads then out and if Tail then in." said George taking out the coin. I wondered he was not afraid of being here, and he threw the coin in the air. With the several turns, that coin traveled back showing its Head part down. Within a second along the flipping of my eyes, I saw those unknown eyes gazing the coin nonstop, opposite to me. Within a while, those eyes disappeared and the coin showed Head side. We remained out.

[What were those powers, Celestial or Manual who saved them? God knows.]

"I am sure this all trickery is done by those eyes alone." I said this confidently.

"How can you say that?"

"No George I am facing it since last month and right now I saw those eyes again."

"It means that manly silhouette is following us." George got the point.

"Yeah and you see we will surely find Veronica and Lial anywhere around us." I said while walking ahead.

"Don't be silly, they are in bus, traveling with others, cool no." George seemed cheese off by our situation.

We reached the end of the lobby, we thought, but it was only the dividing section- parting the other side with the broken doors. We have to pass on the same distance yet. The swaying of ship did not stop; instead, the drizzle through the broken sides drenched us fully. Rapidly, the water coming inside with tremendous force split our hands and we were pushed towards the outer railing. Before gripping anything, we were powerfully thrown out from the ship both one by one. This unexpected blow might have thrown us in that dark water but then how George's wristwatch was tucked with the end of my Stole and I held it tightly, though I leaned out of the railing. George was holding the other end of my Stole that prevented me from going into the water. He rested beside the rod. This all happened in a fluke, not giving a chance to think as well. I was swirling and twisting on the only scarf in this stormy surrounding. George tried his best to lift me up, but the scrawny scarf did not help him, it started tearing itself. Now the only hope was Ganpati Bappa. I closed my eyes tightly and perceived his wide eyes in my mind. Nevertheless, the next moment with the heavy cloudburst George crossed the rod pushing me down towards the water.

"No…o …o …o" nothing could I do than to bawl from my spirit, even George joined me. We hang down above the water only at the strength of torn scarf; it was thrilling. I was first to drop down, holding one end of scarf and the other end roll up around the rod. George seized the middle part of the scarf and swayed on it. I wondered why we did not slump down yet, but… "Herbriea, its Bhattji's 'Taveez' that linger us, see it is fixed with one of the nail beside." George yelled.

Nonetheless the deadly dark, I saw the shade inside the water with its teeny-weeny eyes. It remained in front of me, as if waiting for me to fall down. With the tremendous deluge, again we swayed.

"Hey, what are you doing?" It was George's voice. He said facing upward that proved something fishy above there.

"What is the matter George?" I tried to see there.

"Herbriea, someone is cutting out the scarf."

[Surely, it was those eyes]

"Hey, don't you do this, stupid fellow." I turned my hold and tried to lift up. By the time, he finished his job and I closed my eyes to avoid viewing our plummet… and… at the last minute, some invisible force lifted us and lobbed on the ship's floor again and we were… at last saved… but wait what is this? Oh! No, it wasn't a ship, it was a boat-a simple small boat with two … and this we could see only when the sky filled with the bright rays, patting away darkness from our life.

This was an extreme shock for not finding Kalu with us not even the lobbies and no deadly duel. I was truly shocked and wished to tally with George. Even he looked astounded but enjoying all this. My eyes met with him and we remembered of the savior, but we could not find anyone around except us in the tranquil lake. This seemed to be any vista from any magical movie. O! It is amazing, I am mad about this.

Nevertheless, the savior made us sad; we could not thank him even and he vanished. The secret was yet remained unwrap about his identity. Moreover, we were unable to find the answers to our several queries though we deserve after so much exertion.

Engrossed in thoughts, we finally got nearest to the bank; maybe it was

Mumbai. It was another miracle to reach the vast Mumbai in this tiny boat, moreover alive. George helped me to get down on the land. With a sour heart, we saw the boat moving away from us and after going little far; it vanished into the water.

"I don't feel like going." I said sadly.

"Even me." We agreed on most of the point.

"He was an angel, sent to save us, isn't it?"

"You are right, but who was he?"

"I don't know."

<u>Chap- 10</u>

<u>MUMBAI- the dream city of INDIA</u>

Definitely, it was Mumbai, the muggy wind passing through us filled my nose with the familiar smell of the mud and I felt I had been here many times. I remembered the God Ganesh; it was his hub. I felt excited to step on the land of India's dream city- Mumbai, where to move in was the dream of thousands of people.

The first step on the land of Mumbai, gave rise to the first problem for us- Which way to go and it followed by many others. My fuddy-duddy clock showed 4.00 hrs of evening. Neither hot nor cool wind helped us to move ahead. At the same time, our weak potency demanded for a break. Twirling around we found the place a beach like and got what we needed. We oiled our engine, which it supplied to our brains, too and it worked its best. George tried his side pocket to pay the vendor and I remembered to check mine. With some bucks, Merletta's I.D. card, scalene stones, came out the brochure regarding our tour details. Again, our luck, it seemed, accompanied us.

"Look George, only one and half hr left for our train to take off." I told him looking into the paper.

"Do you know which way the railway station is?" he asked as if I knew everything.

"How could I, I had never been here." I said though not sure.

"I thought they might have mentioned."

"They need not to. We can ask someone."

"That's the only way now." Saying this he approached an old looking man enjoying desert beside, who explained him the route in detail.

The local bus could have carried us there within half-n hour but, our pre-arrival would mystify everyone there and this we wished not.

Therefore, we resolved to walk away the path. It was 'Mumbai central' railway station; we were looking for.

"They might have reached there," I asked George panting and he replied just nodding his head.

After cutting the bushy path towards our dorm from Bhattji, it was not a big deal to walk on a comfortable road for long. In fact, it was more enjoyable.

An attractive malls, sky-scrappers, parks, Multiplexes walked with us and then it was not easy to keep ones head on its place, it moved around. Finally, we reached the famous landmark explained by an old man to George. We spotted inside through its gate. It seemed an oldest theatre opposite to station, showing an Indian romantic movie 'Dilwale Dulhania Le Jayenge' for last seven hundred weeks as it mentioned boldly in the poster. I felt excited even to bypass from there. After a while, crossing the traffic jammed road, we reached station on our sore feet.

"Herbriea, we need to screen ourselves" we reached the platform when George said this.

"How, you better know our luggage was missing and we are alien to this city."

"But you could have taken the remaining along."

"I checked everything, everywhere; nothing was left, George. Only the things present in my pocket were safe." I said touching my pocket full of things.

"Attention students, form a queue orderly" it was Mrs. Sailee's voice, coming from George's backside. We immediately moved towards left, and hid behind the group of passengers standing and peeped to see without being seen.

Mrs. Sailee was ordering the students- our schoolmates to board in their respective coach. They all arrived without our sense, the train as well. It did not looked like in Harry potter; it was the same as other Indian long tour coach with Navy blue body and off-white border on the top bearing the words "Mumbai-Kutch-Mumbai" in black and had no special passengers- all muggles. I realized my chums missed out to share this excitement- to travel riskily but with utmost fun.

"Come on, move fast" again Mrs. Sailee's voice and within a moment, the queue moved jestingly inside the coach and what we see- another Herbriella and George moving with the queue. "Oh my my... look George they seemed to be our identical twins, they ditto look like us. How is it possible?"

"I definitely have no twin brother, what about you?" George asked but regretted when I replied with my sharp eyes. "Uuh... well you are right something fishy is going on." He spluttered. Definitely, not a soul can recognize their pretense. Therefore, they are our replicas who replaced us on purpose, obviously and because of them, nobody bothered our absence.

"George, who are they like us? What could be their aim?"

"Whoever and whatever but it is not fair, let me check them personally." George decisively moved towards them and I just pulled him back through his collar.

"Not now, let them set up." Only just, he restrained. All the students got in, followed by Mrs. Brook and Dr. Teasel. No one was left out, so we swift to get inside the coach just behind and were crashed with Mr. Newman.

"Haven't you heard Mrs. Sailee's instruction?" He asked.

"Err...well..." George tried to answer and I said, "Sir, we were looking for you. Mrs. Sailee asked us to call you."

"Okay, come." He asked us to join him.

"But sir our seat is in S-3 coach and Mrs. Sailee needs you in S-1." I then recognized my mind power, George too. Mr. Newman looked puzzled and we hardly divest ourselves of this situation. T.C. roaming on the platform reminded me about the tickets we had not yet purchased. My worried look made George aware and he took out two tickets from his pocket. It showed our journey to Kutch- Bhuj was certain, though not confirm.

I was busy catching any hidden way through the dividing walls just like in Harry potter when George drag me behind that wall hiding from Veronica and Lial rushing towards their coach. This thrilled me for a while. It was now risky to loiter over there so we walked to our coach S-9 far away from them. "It is so odd." I felt embarrassed finding several eyes on us, perhaps owing to our size. We set ourselves on the seat near to the door when the train took off. The giant clock on the platform showed Five Forty-Five of twilight that means we started ten minutes late then regular time. With the pat of warm breeze, I mull over the prevalence. George remained watching the scene out from the broad window, anxiously. Clanging of metal, screeching of tracks and the bugle of engine showed the tempo of the hustling train. It moved promptly than my thoughts though, my mind tried to stay tuned with it. I truly wished I would have taken that box along, but it was missing too.

Suddenly, I thought of getting into the coach S-3 to console my cranium. George got aware with my movement and we headed towards S-3 coach. All the coaches were connected internally except the A.C coach, so it became easier to roam about.

"Hey kids, with whom you are traveling?" we were asked by a tan Indian woman dressed in sari with two small kids and tons of luggage besides waiting to be arranged to their right place.

"We are from boarding school, Panchgani, going to Kutch with our teachers and friends." George said.

"Shall I help you to find your compartment?" she asked unexpectedly.

"No… No… we'll manage." I said hastily which made her eyes frown and we than left the place.

"You must control yourself," George advised me.

"Yes and let her find our companions too, right." Anyhow, we reached near S-3 coach and slowly moved further hiding ourselves in each possible way. Standing behind the vertical wall, we peeped inside, where after ten- twelve students our replicas were chatting with whom, cannot believe they were Veronica and Lial.

"Oh! They exactly look like us, George." I fussed.

"Right, see that pointed crooked nose, it's definitely yours, isn't it?" he regretted after saying this. I just punched him, but not too hard.

Suddenly from the opposite side came Mrs. Brook counting numbers pointing her finger on each student and then verifying into the paper she held. Behind Mrs. Rao followed her who was giving away the packet of something to each student, maybe evening snacks followed her and I remembered I was hungry. For a while, I strike with a thought of getting those packets at any cost, but the loud sound of ring buzzing somewhere near Mrs. Brook chucked off that idea from my mind.

She started conversing through her mobile. "What? I don't believe! How did it happen? Oh! Jesus, very sad!" her punctuations worried everyone in the coach except our replicas. Mrs. Brook put off the phone very slowly and looked into George's (not real) eyes very sadly. Along with George all of us present there were eager to listen from her. She hesitatingly said, "George… err… your house maid, do you remember 'Akka'… she died today morning." "Impossible!" immediately the words flew out from us. George's eyes and mine too asked the same question that How did she died in the morning when we saw her in the noon for the last time.

"Her neighbor gave this news to your Mum on phone and something else she will tell your Mum in person." Saying this Mrs. Brook closed her eyes and I saw the hellish grin on Herbriella (not real) when she turned her face sideway from Mrs. Brook purposely. I wildly thought of going to Mrs. Brook and making her known to the reality, but this would be again my faux pass. They seemed to possess powers and were able to harm anyone if they wished. Upon all they were unaware about us then why to rise up a beast.

"Can you guess about Akka's message?" asked George in hushed voice.

"No, but it is necessary to know."

"How? It is risky to go there and even dangerous to come back, which is more important." I nodded.

"One possibility is there," he said.

"What?"

"Shhh…" saying this he dragged me towards our coach. We came back to our seat and bought some cuisine called 'Bhel' to make up for our appetite little bit. We gave full justice to the foodstuff looking at the darkness outside the window.

It was dark bushes from where Akka came out and raised her hands towards me. Her big eyes moved briskly as it viewed something behind me. I went watery and turned to see and my head crashed with the sidewall of the moving train through which we were traveling.

 Oh! These nightmares. Very dark, no one was awake not even George sleeping opposite to my berth. I took out my lighthouse and confirmed the time it showed 1.43 of night. I got down from my berth and move towards the toilet without disturbing George or anyone else. Finding something fishy, I moved further and stopped before S-3 coach. My intuition paid me; our replicas were standing in front of an opened door. I again peeped from behind the wall. They stood as if ready to jump and before I could think they spring out of the door. I thought to get hold of them but did not dare. In spite of the dark surrounding I was able to see them rolling down the mound and then vanishing. I rushed back to George and told him everything.

"It's the right time to get back our place." George suggested.

"And even to tell Mrs. Brook."

"Really" and we resolved to move towards S-3 coach.

"We'll get adjusted and make Mrs. Brook aware."

"But George, why did they quit? What did they have on their mind? Bhattji said their main aim was to get me then why they left me?" as usual, I asked him all at once. He opened his mouth to say and the train stopped putting break to our discussion. We reached Ahmadabad station- junction of Gujarat and known as the Manchester of India. Like a magic most of the passengers whom it looked difficult to wake up few minutes ago, just popped out from their berth and rushed to get down first. This disturbed us to move ahead. Some of them hurried to get their water containers filled up, some rushed to enjoy ice-creams for which Ahmadabad was famous and some got up for refreshment. We pulled back our decision and remained in our place. The train was to stay thirty minutes at this station, as usual but the bugle followed by the announcement at the platform attracted everyone to stop their blabbering.

"Attention passengers, we are sorry to inform you that due to some major mechanical problem found in the engine, this train will run after two hours or more. We are sorry for the inconvenience caused to you, Thank you." This led to the tremendous clamor and confusion all over. The people started murmuring more than before.

"So then this was the reason of our replica's exit." George said in my ear.

"George, we must join them now." I was worried to get our identity back. We got up and again tried to get through all chaos around.

The scene in S-3 coach was enough to take the wind out of us. All the students were getting down the train as soon as Mr. Newman called upon their names. They got down with their luggage and provoked me.

"What's the matter? Why all are getting down?" I asked one of my schoolmates.

"You didn't hear? Headmistress had decided to travel further by bus."

"Why? We can wait for two hours." George said.

"No, it is not certain, it may take more time." she said. 'Dipti sachde', Mr. Newman called a last roll a call of sixth class. We got ready for our turn.

As soon as Mr. Newman called our names, we stepped forward but the passengers trying to cut their way to the other side pushed us back on the seats. Somehow, we got up and saw our replicas again with Mr. Newman. God knows! From where did they turn up? They got down and we had to hide ourselves again.

"Oh! Misfate, George only if you had listened to me first." I became furious. He gave me a stupid stare. "Just five minutes before I asked you to go in there and we missed it." I felt like crying.

"Don't be silly, five minutes can't change anything and you know it wasn't my fault." He said rudely and pursed his lips. Only then, we realized the people's eyes fixed on us. This was not the moment to hoard in my mind so I gave it to the people out on the platform. This state did not last long.

"Hey, let's get down." Said George and we did it. It was S-6 coach quite far from them. They all moved towards the exit, we too. George stopped in front of telephone booth and I understood why he was so fraught once we got down.

"Check the time right now. Is it wise to bother her?" I asked him as the time was 3.15 of early morning and the call was to be made within the country.

"Akka's message is the only clue to move ahead." He dialed the numbers and waited. "Pick up Mum… fast." It was obvious to get the answer late owing to an hour. "Mum, George here…"

"…."

"I'll tell you later, first tell me about Akka." then again he waited and listened patiently but became impatient as he went on listening to her. After few seconds when he put down the receiver, he had the mishmash look on his face.

"What happened?"

"It's bad news… Akka's neighbor, whom she gave the message-, died an hour before due to snake bite." I was dumbstruck and could not utter a word.

"She could only say few words to my Mum at her last breathe." I yet could not gather my sense to ask him about those words.

"George's friend should not go to the Palace… these were her last words." George got dishearten. I truly felt sad for Akka and her neighbor and found myself their cause of death.

"Herbriea, isn't it that Palace you have been seeing in your dreams?" George asked changing the sad topic.

"Yes, I think we are on the right track."

"How on the earth would we find the Palace?"

"I don't know; let us find our companions first."

We saw our H.M hiring buses to travel further. It was not difficult to hide ourselves under the cover of darkness but very much necessary to be at thousands arms length from our replica. H.M. hired four buses for all of us and we got into the last one to maintain the distance.

"Hey, you are supposed to accompany your class." Mr. Newman welcomed us reminding our mistake. We had to take the risk to fool him again.

"Yes sir, I had to call my Mum so we got late."

"At this hour?" asked Bijoy a ninth class boy.

"Yeah, I have to tell her our every move without fail, or else you know the Mums... coolest on the earth." And everyone laughed with him. George's statement somewhat satisfied Mr. Newman but it failed before Krisha.Jain of class eighth. She showed her qualm on us. Well, this was the start.

Bus moved with the clap of cool breeze and everyone inside slipped into their dreams. This put us easy with them. I was unable to make my eyelids heavy with my burning stomach and working psyche.

"What do you think George, why the train stopped in the midway?" I did not have the answer from the snoring bull. Dwelling on the entire previous occurrence, even I started dozing and realized only when I ran into the backseat ahead. It was a sudden break laid by the bus in the midst of the lonely dark road. Misfortune leads even more; it happened that the inner lights went out spreading more darkness. Snoring pals woke up and tried to recognize themselves. Despite of the dark, I could see Krisha being more suspicious about her, quite funny.

"What happened sir?" asked one ward from the last row to Mr. Newman just brought the news.

"A bus wheel has got puncture and this has happened with all the three buses too." Oh! Incredible! This went on within the students. Finding some students roaming outside, few from our bus also demanded to go out. Mr. Newman allowed everyone. We were the last to step down, so I turned behind the bus and searched for the baddies but found nowhere. All the teachers and sirs got together at one place.

"There's something on the road to put us up to." Mrs. Brook said.

"Yes, it will take half an hour to mend." Mr. Newman said.

"So then I think we should not allow the children to be out." Miss. Sailee said tamely.

"No Ma'am we won't go in." the students refused going back into the bus. Finding everyone busy with their job, I moved towards the previous buses to… obviously. It was dangerous to walk on the deserted road.

I just have gone few steps ahead when the truck loaded with the people stopped beside us. It seemed they had been to any temple, as each one of them had put a red tikka- a dot on their forehead and were repeating the slogan in their native language. One from the flock asked the matter and Mr. Newman told him our problem. To this, the native started shouting in their Gujarati language. He attracted all the students and we again hide ourselves. Miss. Sailee translated what the man said. According to him, a very old and famous temple was situated in this village just a km in left and to proceed ahead without taking the blessings was impossible. So he advised us to visit this temple first that will help our journey to complete safely. Mrs. Brook pondered for a while and all of us waited for her order.

"Come on, all of you in the bus at once." She ordered and fussed to all teachers. The bus with the help of three unaffected wheels was driven at jet speed and within few minutes, we were in front of the temple. All the students got down but we stayed in to maintain the distance. However, we had to show down when Mrs. Rao called our names repeatedly.

"Why you always create a mess?" she got annoyed. So our replicas flew away again.

"George, now it's whose turn?" I almost murmured.

"Pray to god." He said and moved in.

It was a giant size gate built up in traditional motifs. My first step got me the vibes as I crossed the main door and saw the monkey face God Hanuman about whom I have heard much from my Mum. It was amazing.

According to Indian mythology, Hanumanji were the bodyguard of God Ramji. He was the strongest, bravest of all and very helpful for each living and non-living thing whether on earth, deep inside the water or in the sky. Whoever prayed him heartedly he believed his duty to help him. Praying deeply with my heart I requested Hanumanji not to sacrifice anyone else life at any cost. Suddenly my eyes fell on the board to the deity's right side. So then it is Sarangpur village, famous for curing the complicated cases of black magic, any disable disease and any impossible curse. All this was handled with the God's rod called 'Gada', which was believed to be used by God himself against all evils. All this I knew since my childhood, my Mum had read me many Indian religious stories and explained me thoroughly. She was the greatest fan of the Indian mythology.

The sweet smell of aromatic sticks attracted me towards right outside the temple, where I saw the hut filled with the smoke. All our companions were busy taking blessings so I asked George to follow me and we entered inside the hut.

"Come children, I was waiting for you." An old sage like man welcomed us in his aromatic hut. His pleasure was seen through his eyes. He asked us to sit on the floor in front of him. I wondered how he could speak so fluent English.

"Don't be surprise, I know many languages." He read my mind.

"Sorry, but how did you know we will come here." I asked and he smiled.

"It's his entire wish." He said pointing towards upward. I remembered something and took out the paper from my pocket that Bhattji had given us. Confirmed, he had asked us to visit this same temple and meet Guruji. So this was definitely his wish, oh thank you God.

"You have been sent here, you are unusual, precious for him, for this intact planet and so you are here." He said this devotedly, but I could not take in what he said, in fact I could not believe.

"But it was all just unexpected…" George might have left his mind open, so he tried.

"He never tells anyone about what and how, just walk the way he shows you and you will get on your destiny." George gave him a surprise look but I was suddenly relieved to find someone to escort me correctly. Guruji summoned us nearby and asked us to close our eyes. As soon as I closed my eyes, I felt something penetrating all through my body and became hot within few seconds. My eyes got open and saw Guruji sat still in front.

"It's dangerous but it's the way to your destination. You have to walk on, bravely and for that take this." Saying this he gave me a small metal sheet. Again, I received vibes on touching it. The sheet was plain as playground. Well, I accepted it without giving it a thought.

"This is the most powerful armor presented by God himself to you. It was his wish and I gave you. These are the very powerful ancient signs used in the holy deeds since thousands of years."

"But Guruji there's nothing I can see on it." I examined the sheet from all the sides but found nothing.

Guruji smiled serenely, "Did you ever know you will turn up here at the right time? Had you even thought for that before? Then why you worry now? These signs better know their duty, they will emerge at the right time; just listen to your soul."

"Guruji, something for Me." said George. Guruji smiled "you already have." he said pointing towards George's upper arm where he had tied 'Taveez' given by Bhattji. "I would like you to learn one mantra, if you wish." He said and George nodded. "Okay, say "Jai Hanumanji Mahaveer" whenever you feel danger repeat this until you are safe again."

"Guruji, why am I chosen? Who am I?" I asked the most disturbing question.

"That you will find out…on your own just don't rely on anyone, no matter your dearest ones." Saying this he again slipped into meditation and we got up. We bowed and thanked him and turned out from there. At the doorstep out of the hut, I got one more shining stone. I picked it up to place it in its right place. Coming back in the temple, we were shocked to find none of our folks there. Searching for the buses outside we found them leaving without us… no they did not, they have our replicas with them.

"Herbriea, we must try for the help outside." Said George and found one private car coming towards us. But before George could raise his hand, I pulled him and asked him to travel in S.T. bus instead. Moreover, it was safe and affordable, too.

[A smart decision, they were definitely saved from the weird private car without having anyone for driving it.]

"Can you imagine, George such an unknown game of our fate that we have reached wherever we needed, though weirdly. It was his plan to hinder the train and we travel by road to visit this temple. How it's exciting." I expressed my feelings. Now we had six to seven hours of relief in Bus that it will take to reach Bhuj. George again started snoring, leaving not a single bit of sleep for me. In spite of his snoring, I felt safe with him. He left me alone to chew over lot in my life. The quests Who,

How, Where, What, when, followed by Why? That was more painful. Why, those people died without having concerned with me or they had. This was the most disappointing part of my hurdle. Yet, I knew Hanumanji will definitely solve the crisis of Why, from my life.

We were already awake when our bus stopped at the last station- Bhuj at 11.a.m. and eager to get down for stretching ourselves after so tiring journey. I think I will better travel in train, next time. Next time, why? Come on Herbriea, chuck off this right now. Okay, never- Happy? I was mentally chatting when I saw George getting down without me.

"O, Hello, I think I am with you, Mr. Smith." I said teasing him.

"Yep, but I m sure it's only your thought, Miss. Gold-a dreaming princess." And we laughed. Enjoying this moment we got down. The dusty road where we got down was called Hospital road and the area was called Lal Tekri.

I again went through the brochure; we were supposed to check into the Prince five stars Hotel. There were many shops, two storey buildings and even big showrooms. It looked like a well built up city with all the facilities needed rather the typical village we had expected. However, the proportion of sand that could not purge out from the city was the only left out sign of the village.

"Herbriea, we'll have to hire an auto." George amassed the information we required. I just stared him.

"Well, just dreaming on will not benefit us." Saying this he beckoned one empty, yellow and black, three-wheeler that was called an Auto rickshaw, of course we have learned since we were in Kindergarten. He opt the fare with him.

"You mean by this, this clumsy see how it's blowing sand all around."

"Come on, we don't have to hang out, it offers seats as well." He said getting inside the vehicle. Apart from the concrete buildings, some of the natives here reminded of any village- a serene village.

"One thing George, how did Akka knew that I was enchanted?" I asked him when he was looking at the storm of dust swirling outside.

"Well… from Bhattji she said."

"How can Bhattji know about me, where as he had never seen me before."

"He might have given her any clue or say any mark."

"Exactly, but what mark? It was preferable to ask Bhattji, when we met." I realized George was irritated.

Within few minutes our Auto stopped little away from the hotel Prince. The crowd around it holds us back to proceed. There were few khaki dressed men talking to some boys and girls dressed in beige formal suit. They looked from a similar group, as the woven red badge on the left side of their formal coat denoted so. Without waiting for George, who was paying an Auto fare, I slide through the crowd in the midst. A rabble around looked aggressive. The main door of the Hotel was closed and sealed with the help of many tapes; this showed something had happened here. I looked upon one pale man from the crowd and asked, "What's the matter Uncle?"

"You are not supposed to roam about. I've arranged for you in another Hotel." Instead of that man, the answer came from my back. I turned and saw a hefty from belly, half-bald and darker than coal, man stood with a suspicious look in front of me. He scanned me from top to bottom. I wonder who he so dominant was.

"I asked your teachers to check into Lakeview Hotel. Haven't you gone there?" I was puzzled and wished him to say more.

"But sir..."

"Herbriea... shall we leave now?" George cut me short. He held my arm and literally dragged me out from the crowd.

"What are you doing stupid; he'll come to know everything." He said scolding me. We didn't stop walking the footpath, in fact; he took me far away from the sight of the Hotel.

"Sorry, I know you were trying to sort out the reason." He said very carefully. "It was like a girl had check in here with her parents last night. She lost her control and caused a massive damage to the set up of Hotel. She is being cursed severely says some natives, but the authorities denies it. All this happened today early morning before our arrival. So the Manager of this Hotel arranged another Hotel for us. But the same case repeated in Lakeview Hotel compelled us to shift in Dharamshala, situated out of the vicinity of the Bhuj." George said these in one breathe.

"Dharamshala, what's that?"

"It's a place where visitors can stay for eight-ten days at reasonable cost and limited facilities, but being all the Dharamshalas of the Bhuj already booked we've been shifted far away."

"Why, we could have gone to any other Hotel here."

"No, nobody wishes to live on fire."

"I am the root cause and I've to stay on the bank, it's hurting." George gave me hanky to wipe out my tears.

"George, it's a threatening sign for us."

"Yes, he doesn't want you to reach there, so Herbriea please... don't cry." He said caringly.

"George, you don't let me miss my chums, thanks." I realized how it was difficult for one to express their feelings in person.

We walked down the street that led us to a deserted dusty lane with the small huts both the sides. It again gave me the same feeling I had experienced on the Ganesh Visarjan day, a silent wind spinning with the sand with no life.

"George, why are we here?"

"A native has explained me the shortcut towards the Dharamshala." He said moving his head.

"But it ends up here and there's no way further."

"Well, let's see." George was not sure about the native, but I trusted him. After a while we noticed that not only the lane, the huts were deserted, too, when we approached two-three huts to ask about the shortcut if any. Anyways we walked down the sloping lane until end. The giant wall in front of us seemed to be the end, but the broken door of the last hut in the left and the rays coming out through the backside wall showed the way in. Entering inside we saw the roof being half broken, few earthen vessels being smashed and looked the spick and span being disturbed on purpose. The rays of the sun peeped in through the bamboo wall and we moved towards it. We tried to peep back and felt the heat as well. Touching the bamboo rod, they willingly lay down and we were slapped by the hot dusty wind. Amazing! It wasn't a sand bed for one- but for thousands – a typical real desert, we have read in our books- a Desert of Kutch. So we were supposed to cross this, how?

"Now this could not be the shortcut." I said tiredly.

"Yes, it is." He stamped on my words.

"Hope you won't let me to get there on just four feet." I doubt we can travel like caravans.

"Then how about eight feet." He said with his dancing eyes on the mammal far approaching towards us. The next moment we set ourselves contentedly on the ship of the desert- a Camel. However, we had no powers like Harry and Hogwarts to help us yet we were definitely moving within the magical veil. One would never realize we had not ridden a Camel; it was just simple as riding a bicycle without moving our hands and legs. I have always heard about the horrible heat in the desert and the same we were experiencing.

I saw the waves of sand moving towards us and regretted to sit ahead of George. The waves continued and stopped at the sight of those two eyes again. The hump of camel made us nod and that silhouette vanished again. So he chases us, I guess.

"George, can you imagine the sand having waves?" I asked him.

"Ah…well, not sure." he said frowning.

"Then how about an ice-cream?"

"Oh, sure Mrs. Brook will serve us better." And we laughed. It was not easy to travel in desert without any shade for long but thank god! We had a ride. Secondly, it was a shortcut… was it. I wonder. The swirling wind did not allow the sand to rest and it too moved vigorously.

"Something's gonna be wrong." Suddenly I said.

"What?"

"See even the sand's shade proves that." I said pointing towards the darker sand than the one we passed by.

"Come on it has some scientific reason we have already studied." We were totally exhausted and thirsty too.

"George, we have learned about an oasis too." I said tiredly. He looked around the lonely desert, "Over there" and pointed towards the down slope, where the blue patch was seen in the midst of the black sand. He tried to move the camel towards it, but he did not move. George tried his level best and that silly nut went on denying.

"Oh, this is tough." Finally George tried to stop him, as though it was a signal for the creature, he hasten not letting us to get down and we saw the pond passing away from us, helplessly.

[With the cyclone of the sand swirling above the pond Herbriella and George could not see the flapping tongues trying to come out from the lake.]

Our compelled ride stopped only at the obstruction of an American woman in Indian traditional dress up. Tall approx, six feet height, very fair, long blonde braid of her curly hairs lay in the front trying to reach her waist, were decorated with colorful buttons, her small eyes with black liner dripping out from the eye corners, short round nose and short dark lips, long traditional earrings swaying on every blow of wind, same patterned necklace, dozens of bangles in both the hands, richly adorned fingers with rings. "Oooff! What a traditional beauty." Said George and I pinched him. Leaving out her hairs and features, she was a perfect example of Indian native of Kutch, until she spoke.

"So you are back, Hellebore." She said this directly onto my face.

"Well…" she gestured to keep quiet towards George whose mouth then remained open.

"GACHHATI SAMAPAYATI TAV KARYAM." She told this to me again. My eyes showed my awareness to her tongue, but she gave mulish look and asked our ride to move on. And this was better right now. Very slowly we moved.

I had the better chance to get down at once and know everything from her but something didn't allow me. Maybe the thought of her need in future led me to check the surroundings. Many small tents were built up in a very big spacious place, alike to playground. Smoke coming from most of the tents swirled with the wind out and disturbed the sand, too. With this the delicious smell spread out and showed their lunchtime approaching, definitely it was. Despite of prickly heat we were cold to touch.

"Do you know her?" asked George as soon as we left the deserted area.

"Of course, she is my cousin sister and we lived together in Tanzania."

"What, When?"

"A…approx ten years ago."

"Hey you kidding, okay what's your age now." He asked frantically but fused down on my wild stare. The drops of sweat drenched us as we came into the inhabitant's area. Other vehicles too followed us now. The stubborn camel did not yet stopped.

"George, we must now ask someone about the Dharamshala."

"How, this creature is not ready to stop."

"Oh, then try out your styles." I just provoked him. Suddenly he lifted his left leg from the side and placed it beside his right.

"What are you doing, George?"

"Trying my styles..."

"Don't do this; you'll be crashed by the vehicles following."

"Nothing doing." Again, the speed of the mammal increased and George acted upon his words.

"No... don't." these were my last words to have reached him. I too jump down that threw me in the thorny bushes beside. Thank god for not letting us crush under the tempo of the wheels. Patting the bony parts of my body, I got up to look for George around...

"Hugh...my knee..." we had to pay a lot to get rid of that creature, I thought rubbing my knee.

Hardly two steps I had gone ahead when I stumble on the heap of dry grass mask on a woody thing having textures. "Ahhhhh..." a long cry followed by the grassy monster like made me to sprint backside. It was George, wiping his elbow, looked like a vegetative angel {or Joker}. He got annoyed as I tried to hold back my snicker.

"Who told you to jump after me?"

"Than what, I had to follow your styles." My accent shake while hiding out the fun I was feeling.

"I thought of finding the way to stop that creature."

"With this?" I pointed his bleeding elbow and knees. We were surrounded by the thorny bushes and were unable to find the way out. *Suddenly the spreading up of the roots reminded me of my nightmare that I visualize in front of both the Ma'am. The realistic scene in front was similar to that. Same wild roots stretch themselves flowing out the red blood. It grew out from downward and elongate upward covering us from the open sky. The ambush made its grip tight and was going to grab us when just breaking apart the all difficult bushes, that mammal, that camel, that creature turned up just like an invisible car in Harry Potter and like a miracle the thorny bushes pulled back. Savy the Superhero- the camel saved us and bind us to ride on him.*

"Oh, not again." George said nervously.

"Hey dude, dyou know our destiny?" I asked our savior. He shook his head in care and I felt he would take us the right way to the right place. He again sat down and I asked George to follow me.

"See Herbriea, this time I am not going to jump" he said and something fussed in the Camel's ear on which Savy stamped his forelegs as such that it would definitely blew away George with the sand. George had to run from there to save him. Finally, he sat behind me and saved me from revealing my chuckle.

"Why, what did you say to him?"

"He is impossible, I just requested him to behave like a gentleman and see what he did." At the last, I could not hold myself and burst out of laugh. We continued with our curtailed journey accompanied by warm dusty wind.

"It was clever to take Gog's along." Saying this George took out his sunglasses and offered me. On my refusing, he put it himself.

Life on the road slowed down due to excess heat, I think. After passing away the jungle of concrete, the sight of green and fresh farms cooled our eyes. That showed the village area began. With the help of warm weather though, I started detecting the Sanskrit words spoken by the Indo-American woman we met. Before George could ask me anything new about her, I wished to trace those words.

The peasants were found resting beneath the thickest tree and having their late lunch with their family. The life here seemed to be so simple and sober. Small children were playing while eating and looked relieved without any mental stress. I could not hope for such a serene life, as I knew I was on the way to many complications, many restless days and nights. Only the relief with me was George, yes I was with him.

The Tree house

[The climate started changing, whichever places Herbriella and George passed away. They found the new way to life, new flowers bloomed out, old one became again young, tall trees started dancing on the rhythm of bushes and lawns beside, the wind seemed to sing with the birds flying in joy from one tree to another. The Butterflies flew as though they just found their lost wings and tricked the children trying to catch them. All this was amazing and was definitely a sign of something very special dear things to happen. Unaware of these beautiful feelings Herbriella and George moved on the Camel's wish]

Many signboards denoting the places were left behind until now, but the mammal did not wished to turn on any of them. Cannot say how much we have traveled and yet how much to go. We left Bhuj city far behind, the board now visible showed the name 'Mandavi', the sign of arrow was turned in right side, and distance of two km was written at the base that means it was two kilometer ahead. We hoped our ride to turn at least there and end this weary journey.

"Now if it doesn't turns here than see what I am going to do." said George furiously.

"What?" I asked and laughed thinking of our foolish try to shun this helpful mammal. Suddenly the smarty Savy turned left towards the tapered lane covered with thorny bushes from both the sides. It was quite before the turn of 'Mandavi'.

"Hey silly… sorry… smarty dude are you sure…oh hope so…" George could not keep his mouth shut.

"George, you know my reason of being here, but you didn't say yours." I asked him which I was supposed to ask him before starting our journey.

"Many reasons have bound me to come here. First for education purpose, secondly the fun that we have with our friends, thirdly you are my friend with me and lastly..." thinking for a while he said, "That's all."

"Don't lie, tell me the last one."

"Christina, my sister. I was too small that time, but now I want to find out the reason."

"But you said it was earthquake..."

"But I don't believe so." As soon as we, started chatting the Savy slowed down his speed, as if, trying to keep ear on us.

"Herbriea, you found those scalene stones on the procession day right."

"Only one, second one I found lying on my floors lobby, when I saw that unknown man's silhouette for the first time and the third one you know, I found at the door step of Guruji's math."

"Two more you got in Merletta's room right."

"Yes and meditating I saw all the stones together joining and forming into a petal shape."

"What type?"

"Dusty brown."

"Really, but I've never heard about this color of flower."

"So you think it's a flower petal, you didn't say you've switched on to Biology from Sports."

"Why, an Athlete doesn't have the heart?"

"No I doubt them having the brains." I felt his irritation through his silence.

"George, the strange thing I saw in Mouzami's drawer, it was Merletta's badge which she had lost on the next day of procession."

"What's strange in that? Merletta might have left there by mistake."

"No, she can't, I know she had never been to Mouzami's room. Well, I think it was Veronica, you remember when Merletta came in search of her badge and was followed by Veronica."

"How can she do that?"

"She needs to know everything about me always. She might have stolen from innocent Merletta and hide it in Mouzami's drawer."

"Is that so easy?"

"For her anything's easy. You know her fan followings, any one of them have done for her."

"Why will she do that?"

"She jealous me and will do anything to madden me."

"Okay, then why Mouzami didn't tell you."

"All this happened out of her sense when she went for exams. Veronica did this after finding her powerful friend pairing with me; she couldn't bear this and did it out of frustration."

"Your stories won't do well, you took her amiss."

"Oh come on, you better know her."

"Herbriea, you can't blame her for all your complications."

"I can… at least after seeing her chatting with our replicas in train or else nobody on earth could have made Herbriella to sit with Veronica, impossible." I angrily stamped my leg and realized hurting unnecessarily a silent creature.

[Still Herbriella and George were unknown with the drastic change in the climate around them. Greenery popped out even on unfertile land and the flight of Butterflies followed them. Birds flew from one tree to another as though watching out their movements and wind became a messenger gradually informing their arrival further. Underground roots stretched up to welcome a special visit whereas Herbriella was still busy in recalling her past just few months ago.]

"Do you remember, while playing 'Harry Potter and the philosophers' stone', she spoke the Malfoy's dialogue against Hermione that was I and bashed Stephen backstage." George did not say anything.

"And that day dyou know, I got detention because of her from Math's teacher and Mrs. Brook railed me in addition."

"Mrs. Brook didn't scold you. She just cut out marks from your house, Herbriea."

"That's what I mean."

"Anyway, you owe her your life during our football match and that counts more."

"Yes, of course and then she handed me that beautiful bouquet to name me Black sheep in front of all the girls."

"Well..."

"Now enough, I don't want her to take over me." George kept quiet but the fire rose inside me was unable to put off. Suddenly I felt a very cozy touch on my shoulder; it was George of course and then I remember Guruji's advice to control myself and to turn my weakness in strength. I, too thought, it was worthless arguing with George, when he was not in any of the issue against me.

When did the sun set out along with his last single ray, we did not realized. Dull pinkish sky moved with us on the way that was now deserting. I wondered why our ride was not speeding up and why George was not getting on nerves. It was obviously my mistake. I think I must...

"Sorry... George."

"What?"

"I shouldn't have been so harsh."

"So then you..."

"Don't ask me to let off Veronica."

"Okay, don't just stamp him next time; give him on my behalf also." He said pointing towards the Camel and we cheered up again. I remembered my chums and about the fun, we had always being together.

This region was a typical village with not enough of lights and not many people on the street. After certain distance a row of lights were seen far in the sides of the way we were moving.

"One thing is sure; the thing that is after you was the same cause for Kesar, Liz, Akka- her neighbor, and Gopi."

"Yes, George and now I remember that the cause behind spoiling of Sanskrit book was the same, as he did not want me to find that."

"Oh, yeah than how did you get that woman's tongue?"

"Whose? I don't know about whom you are talking." I ignored him hoping he will drop out the topic and it happened.

Abruptly, a very sensitive current passed throughout my body and my head turned left where far in the bushes I felt something fishy. George got me and followed my reaction. A sigh of relief came out from us when a black cat jumped out of the thick bushes, maybe chasing her prey to satisfy her wintry appetite.

[Who was chasing whom, Herbriella was unaware of this, but one knows the other world was on fire on every further step of Herbriella towards her destination. So then the measures were taken, teams were marched up to finish the work left incomplete a Century ago.]

Unexpected, incredible thunderclaps with lightening are never welcome when they are unseasoned. However, it had become a habit to cope with these bizarre situations. The Camel tried to walk under the shade proving him the most responsible caretaker. Nevertheless, one pleasant surprise- no single drop of rain pours down despite these thunderclaps.

[It was out of Herbriella and George's sense that the unseasoned thunderclaps with lightening emerged on purpose and could harm them any moment. Next moment the effect started and the deadly sparkles aimed the selected. It could hardly cut the air when the strong limbs of giant trees on the either side of the street, stretched up high to form a roof above them. The deadly sparkles failed to cut the roof which was armor to Herbriella and George.]

"Oh I think we are going to reach now." I said seeing the mammal speeding up.

"Don't dream, it's his style." George said patting the Camel caringly.

[Getting no chance to grab its prey, the shattered sparks became furious and decided to strike with intent. Again, it called on the thunderclaps to its help and instead of its prey it assaulted the archaic stone lying within the thorny bushes from when, nobody knows. The determination of the spark resulted in the breaking apart of it and the statue of flapped tongue crop up from the broken stone. It came to life at once, leaking the deadly drop. The drop in turn made the bushes on the ground to shrink and thorns to thrive and gave spaces to the biggest flower, odorless, Raflesia. Tremendous thunderclaps welcomed her and the sparks hopped around rejoicing. It was not the celebration, but it was a challenge and was bravely accepted by the warriors of this world. In fact they had been awaiting this for long and for their true descendant. They too marched their teams, the roots of the entire trees in the surroundings stretched and moved along with every ensuing step of Herbriella and George.]

"At last, we reached" seeing more lights and houses, George said this. Getting little closer we saw the houses built up in a row, unlike any village huts and looked definitely like Dharamshala.

"Hey, dude…is you okay?" George shouted on the Camel who without stopover turned in the wrong lane and swiftly stopped only in front of the giant tree. I lifted my head and was surprised to see a crooked weird house instead of the tree I had seen from far away. "Impossible… it wasn't a hut … it was a tree." It really looked like a tree with green colored roofs and rusty brown walls.

"George… did you see this, how is it possible?"

"Oh! Not again."

"No you see there was no house. I saw here a giant tree awhile ago… I swear." I said this panting a lot.

"It happens… we are in desert."

"No George I tell you."

"Whatever you say, but this is the safest place until we find them."

"Why? You said we will tell everything to Mrs. Brook and she will help us out."

" she is going to believe us in the presence of our replicas? And we need to dig out their intention."

"I think you are right."...As soon as we got down, our ride disappeared as though it was not there. Before George can knock the door, it opened itself and no one welcomed us. Once we entered, I heard the rustling of trees together; the smell of fresh greenery overflowing my nose, and the things inside the house seemed to move once. A weird but beautiful house was spacious from inside with almost all the necessities though old fashioned. Again, I met with my dream in person. There were steps to climb up and a room to sleep in. The well-furnished double bed raised our covetousness to have a nap but then it also reminded of our empty stomach. Nevertheless, before everything, we wiped out the wounds we got and cleaned ourselves thoroughly, though we had no fresh clean clothes to put on.

"Everything's perfect. Might we find something to eat? C'mon." I suggested and we again climbed down towards Kitchen.

"What would you like to have, Senorita?" asked George dramatically.

"Oh, a grill sandwich with French fries and Pizzas with extra cheese...I think that will be okay." I too replied him in the same manner. As we step down, the smell of pizza bread and frying chips led us to kitchen quickly. And we saw the plates kept on the dining table were already served with delicious Sandwiches and Pizzas, just like in Snow white story, Wow wonderful! Now we had no one here to interrupt, so we just fall on the cuisine. It was not wise to be so careless, I know, but you can't expect one to be civilized after he has starved for the days. We ate at our full content and when I tried to discuss our aim, George just went to sleep. In spite of extreme weariness, I could not shut my eyes. No, I was not worried for the place; though it was just a day shelter but I felt my home here. I know it was new yet familiar, more energetic, fresher, and touchier, and definitely I will find my destination too. It's gorgeous feeling and does not know how long it will last… I was definitely tired after so long…but the brightness of moon peeping inside attracted me to sight the only hope among the darkest surroundings…

Dharamshala

Crowing of cock woke me early in the morning. Bright sunrays peeped inside through the cracks of the window and I just leapt to see the village's natural beauty I opened the only woody window and felt the fresh air on me. There was a giant banyan tree in the backyard by the fence. The scene around the tree was really cool. Sparrows were busy gossiping on the tree, pigeons were least bother about them, they were silently having their breakfast spread on the ground and the crows were giving their ear to sparrows at a time and the next moment irritating the pigeons by sharing their food. I was even lucky to hear the dawn chorus. This was truly the scene I craved to see, it just drew me deep. However, the heavy music of George's snore pulled me back in the room. It was now time to get ready and check Dharamshala, I thought. I tried to wake up George but he was not ready to leave his comfort. So finally, I did what he deserved. "O...O.o.sh what's this?" George sprint out of the bed, wiping all the water I had put on him.

"It's my style, dude." I said jestingly.

"Oh, you silly girl, I was about to solve the mystery and you..." he said rubbing his eyes.

"Now it's time to solve our real life mystery, Sweetie."

"Hey, don't you call me that." His nose with his cheeks turned pink and looked even sweeter.

"Okay, dear then get up, it's the show time now." I said robustly.

"Aaaahn..." but the lazy boy just yawned.

"Don't do that." I fling a pillow on him and he threw back, I curl down briskly and the pillow fell on the side panel of the woody window and within no time, the metal railing pulled out with innumerable attire, which made George bounce from the bed. He just rushed to find out the

best for him and even I tried few. When we finished selecting, I did not
missed to find out the origin of railing but couldn't. It was like we got
what we needed, a magic or... whatever. Obviously, it is his entire wish.
*[The Golden touch of sunrays shone every bit of the tree house as bit by bit
it habituated with its cute visitors. It was the utmost feeling of fresh
pleasant day. However, the share of Golden touch is equal for every living-
non-living things on the earth…whether they are Good or... Little far away
in the thorny bushes, the biggest flower of the world- Raflesia widen out
and drip down the drop of its sweat which fell on the statue with the moving
tongue and got the life throughout its body. "It's the time to work now."
Same callous voice came from the just bloomed flower and it moved with
the strong deadly determination. The statue remained no more still. It came
to life fully and got ready to finish his incomplete task over century ago.]*
"George, we got to go now." I told him once we had shower and dressed
up in new cloths. George like an obedient collected all our belongings [we
hardly had any] and accompanied me out of the tree house holding my
hand.
"Miss. Herbriella, you don't need me. See, he is at your service." He
said as we found our ride standing at the front of the half-broken fence.
"Don't be silly, he is just helping us."
"Helping, or harassing."
"Whatever, and because of him you were at ease at least a night."
"Right, it was just like a bracing up a Sheep for deliberate carnage.
Okay, if you wish Madame, anything for you." He bowed again.
"But…just tell your well wisher not to stamp sand on me… and not
to…" his words flew in the air as I dragged him out on the lane.
Dharamshala was just the next lane, so we did not ride the camel but he
followed us. We climbed the backside wall as it was risky to get in
through the front gate. The closely packed trunks of the Banyan and the
Peepal trees covered us while climbing. The small row houses had the

two floors with the flat roofs like any city built up. However, the small narrow section connected the other row house. We were confused to start, exposing ourselves may lead us to never ending trouble, so we decided to depart and check out from different directions. At the time of early dawn, the nature was at its best with calm and cool climate, I would never wish to miss out. But the job on mind forced me to find out those who have made my life restless. I turned left and went on, as all the houses were built in circular row connecting each other. We both together found eight row houses with a vast circular space in the middle. "No one is awake." George said.

"Shall we check their rooms?"

He went towards the main gate.

"Why, you said it's risky." I asked him.

"Yes it is and we'll have to take it." He said bravely and we moved on. *[Their brisk movement attracted Veronica and Lial stood in the window of the second floor. Veronica lean more to see them and grinned hellishly.]* The shove of cool wind helped us to reach there quickly. We saw the iron doors of the gate was locked from inside, so our school was yet sound slept. We now faced the Dharamshala. We waited awhile for someone to appear but no sign.

"I think they are not here." I said.

"How can you say that? Let's go, we'll have to ask someone." Said George asking me to follow him in just when I heard the sound of lock getting open behind us. Immediately I turned but found no one in or out of the gate, though it was left open.

"What happened?" asked George. I showed him the opened gate. We moved towards it. George pulled in the door, stepped out and checked all the sides, if anyone had escaped after playing a prank with us. Not even a single bird was found to be passed from there and then I saw the Gorgeous Royal Gate, exact opposite. It looked an ancient antiquated art of the time. Definitely, I was dragged towards that artifact. The dusty road had no one to walk on except me, yes; George was bound to follow me. Almost half of the gate's side was covered with soft and fresh bushes. The upper rim and the side pillars were carved in specific traditional designs and the doors were carved in small motifs of warrior Elephants and Horses. The Peacocks too, enhanced the beauty of the doors. This panorama rouse out my inner artistic soul and I wished not to move out from there.

"What are you doing here?" Mrs. Rao's voice asked us and before turning to her, my mind started working on the story we'll have to cook up. She stood with the unknown man looked like a Guard and was giving us a surprise look.

"No use to ask you how did you got here, right." She taunted. She waited, but I said nothing, not even George; maybe he was pondering like me. And the problem was that we were traveling with them whereas we were not.

"Oh Herbriea, why are you so tough, I don't understand." Again cursing me, she turned inside and asked us to follow her. There was no time to think hundred times before entering inside the Dharamshala. I held George's hand, closed my eyes and without thinking deep, I took a step further. Suddenly I heard the sound of door getting open behind me. I opened my eyes and turned back to prove my sharp mind. I asked George to see there, so that I should not look stupid again. But he proved me so. He didn't see what I saw and we were carried inside with great care. Mrs. Rao could not help her head to turn back on our each moving step. I think she doubted on our decision to get in. The scope found empty few minute ago was filled with the students all around. It looked like whole Minerva Boarding school being shifted here. Some of the pupils were heading towards the second house from the left. The reason to go there at this hour infer to the breakfast venue. Even Mrs. Rao got in there and left we out with the confusion whether to follow her? I could not yet chucked off the thought of that gorgeous gate opened just for me, so I was not prepared to find the way out. George pulled my hand and took me behind one thick tree.

"Screen your face Herbriea."

"Why?"

"We have not found them, yet"

"But this will not pay us; instead we must get in the second house and face what comes." We both had the brains and the tuning. George was persuaded and we came out when... "SURPRISE" a loud familiar voice followed us. Seeing the owners of the voice, the words flew out from me as well, "Whoopee... How are you here?" I hugged my best chums Mouzami and Nanisha and didn't felt like leaving them. They were the greatest cause of my happiness today. "Mouzami, it's amazing to see both of you here, but how did you fall across." I was not able to hide my jest.

"No... it was..."

"Oh come on, let us get oiled first." Said George before Mouzami could complete her sentence.

"Herbriea, you said he talks about food all the time and not the oil." It was difficult to explain Nanisha and even to avoid George's wild stare. So I briskly headed towards the second house, where the huge dining hall on the ground floor was packed with the Minerva students. We found the right place for us and got relieved for nobody staring us weirdly, though George has to bore Veronica's brutish stare with every morsel of Dhokla and Chutney [A famous Gujarati dish] There were Upama, Sheera, Thepla and much more mouth watering dishes. Too many delicious cuisines waited to get into my stomach but it was already full with my chums' arrival and my heart eager to get empty.

<u>Bunnie-the victim place</u>

"Now what's next?" asked Mouzami after we had our breakfast.

"Wait, first listen to me." and then I told them everything about the crisis I fought with the help of George.

"So it was our right decision to come here, canceling our trip to Delhi." Nanisha said.

"Where, Delhi!" asked George. "Oh, it's the same place famous for having wonderful Palace 'Taj Mahal'- one of the Seven Wonder of the World, right." George said eagerly and I wonder his interest in social studies, too.

"Mouzami, why did you canceled your trip?" finally I asked her.

"We phoned George's Mum yesterday to know your whereabouts, she told us everything she knew and immediately we decided to come here. Our Parents got Mrs. Brook's permission and they brought us here."

"They left?"

"No, they will travel around Kutch instead of Delhi now."

"Mouzami, Nanisha did you come to meet her before you left on your trip?" asked George pointing towards me.

"No, our parents had already booked the tickets for Delhi, so we had to leave instantly. It was too fast and we could not even inform you, Herbie, we are very sorry for that." Mouzami and Nanisha apologized and I felt to hug them again.

"It's okay, but then where were you those three days?" I could not believe that they were not physically present with me and that was my illusion.

"We had been to Mumbai, did shopping and were about to fly Delhi, but your Mum's call changed our decision." There was a bit silence awhile.

"Oh, George you are so wonderful." Suddenly I hugged him to have such a wonderful mother. All of them got baffle with their mouth open. Even I felt embarrassed.

"Okay, first let's find out our rooms." Nanisha said taking us out from the embarrassment, unknowingly.

"Oh wow, so you are going to stay with us?" I asked excitedly.

"Yes of course, why to miss such a golden chance." They equally were excited.

"Hey, George you are wanted." Rustin yelled while coming towards us.

"Why?" George asked.

"You forgot to close the tap in Mr. Apte's bathroom. Good job dude." Rustin said this finding it a fun; Ronak also accompanied him.

"No, when?"

"Weren't you with him last night?" Ronak asked suspiciously and we all exchanged an understanding look.

"Oh really, oh yeah… err well … it was Mr. Apte's bathroom?"

"Oh c'mon, don't tell me, he had called you to know the secret of your special talent, so what have you did there?" asked Bill appearing from backside.

"What talent?" George asked.

"Now flapping the tongue alike a serpent, won't you call this a special talent?" said Ronak.

"And I bet nobody can do this better." Rustin said. We started boiling in the hot water.

"What's new, haven't you seen Discovery channel?" said George hiding his expression.

"But really it was outstanding, you are just superb." Rustin said chuckling with other guys. We all stood dumbstruck and they were laughing as though it was a part of George's prank.

"Anyway, he wants to see you, immediately."

"Where?" George asked randomly.

"Now tell us, you don't know your room too."

"Hey, have you got your memory elapsed?" Rustin asked sharply throwing a sharp look on me.

"Oh! George you have totally changed…" Rustin left his advice incomplete keeping me in his sight.

"George, c'mon fast," bellowed Smitesh from the gate of building no. four and we got George's shelter.

Veronica's arrival has never been liked… as she appeared, all the George's friends moved away but George was held up again.

"Why you haven't got any manners or lost it on someone?" we can never expect any good from her.

"Why, What for?"

"Why… cause' I beckoned you and what, for you were leaving so early with this useless." George was great to take this in, clenching his teeth. We were bound to view this.

"But Veronica, I didn't see you."

"Obviously." Said Veronica again squinting at me

"Veronica, we have patched up and unless…" I tried to help George but…

"Unless… unless Mrs. Brook had not forced me, I would've never accompanied you in the train and I definitely regret for that… you…Hugh." And suddenly she burst out of laugh when she saw my chums. "Afraid right? You always need support… delicate coward." Saying this she briskly moved away. So she knew I was talking about the train amity which she had crop up with our replicas unknowingly or… and the cause behind this was Mrs. Brook… definitely Mrs. Brook was unaware. I know she has always advised me to be friendly to all creatures on this earth… but what if some of them are wacky like…

"So it hadn't stopped yet." Nanisha said this.

"Never going to end." I said helplessly.

"George you must go now."

"But what about your room?" he was truly worried.

"We'll find out." I said with confidence and raised my hand but he did not respond and moved away silently. I knew he was hurt.

"What's the matter?" Mouzami asked after he left.

"It's always Veronica, don't you know?" anyway let us find out mine. We checked all the buildings to decide which one to approach first.

"Helbliella." I thought my ears going passionate nowadays, but it was a real Merletta to give me second most shock.

"Whele have you went today molning, I called you when you wele standing at the gate." And I thought our secret entry was yet hidden, where as it is being publicized.

"Oh! Merletta, even you are here?"

"What ale you saying?" she looked puzzled.

"Merletta, she means what you are doing here, down and actually we… we two didn't know you were allowed to this trip." Mouzami handled her.

"Oh, she knows this." She pointed at me. "It was Mls. Blook, being so kind, she did not mind when I climbed into the Bus, by mistake. I was hiding out of feal, so they came to know aftel leaching midway and she allowed me." This increased my respect towards Mrs. Brook.

"So kind of her." Nanisha said ardently.

"Helbliella, youl belongings ale messed up, I came to tell you this." On this I remembered my only belongings in my pocket was safe and the cloths which were not mine, I had not carried from the tree house and now this new luggage …surely…Merletta was talking about my replica… in fact all of them were talking the same. So it was done, our replicas are not present right now and this chance we must grab it.

"Come Merletta, come with me." I followed her. Besides it was a good idea to know my room. She led us to one on second floor in building no.

eight nearest to the gate. It was a single room for six pupils and only a cupboard to share. Merletta showed me the things, which were scattered beside the open door of the cupboard. My favorite pink pinafore and blue trouser and white polo neck T-Shirt and black checked hanky …hanky? Oh! It was the same swelter cloth I found in the library…but I had kept it in my antique box… Oh No, that means my box is too stolen. I moved my head around but could not find it. "Hey, isn't that same cloth…" I immediately put it into my overloaded pocket "Sh...Sh..." and curbed Nanisha to continue. So our replicas have had a better chance. "What happened?" asked Merletta seeing my shrug.

"Ah…well its nothing, thanks dear." She smiled and hugged me. She was easily convinced. Nanisha did her job and checked our neighborhood. "There's Mrs. Sailee and some of your class mates." I was not at all bother for whom was to the next door, for the feeling of joy surpassed me on returning to my place and hoped George too gets his. However, the next moment, Mrs. Sailee came in clapping and saying, "Come on girls, we are getting late. Herbriella, haven't you bathed yet… and what about you both… well I think you were not with us…right?" she doubted on my chums.

"No Ma'am, but we have taken Mrs. Brook's permission."

"It's all right, but you can't stay in this room. It is already full."

"But… Miss…"

"No, nothing doing. I will arrange for you above the dining hall, there is a single room. Come follow me." and my chums again left me unwillingly.

"Helbliella, go get leady, we have to go to see the victim aleas." And she brought my mind to the actual aim of our being here. It was our educational trip and we were bound to follow Mrs. Brook wherever she wishes to take us. I thought it better to take shower again and put on new fresh clothes. So I picked my favorite pink pinafore and waited outside the fresh room to get vacant. Three of my classmates were busy packing the needful for the journey, I guess.

"Herbriella, have you noted down yesterday's report?" asked Aayushi.

"Well, I didn't have any paper with me so I couldn't." It was better to lie, rather than expecting them to believe my real but incredible story.

"How are you going to make the projects then?" she again asked.

"I thought of borrowing, if you don't mind, thanks for reminding." Neelam tore some papers from her book to lend me.

"Can you do me one more favor?" I requested and they all agreed.

"I forgot yesterday's spot, can you give me the details that you have collected."

"Sure, yesterday we had gone to 'Anjar' village. But I can help you only after I finish writing it." Deepali said.

"O.k. a.y" I wished to dig out the palace in any of the places we had or we will go, anyway...

"And today we are going to 'Bhachau' right?" I supposed as I found this the most affected village while going through the net.

"No, it's 'Bunnie'." The answer came from the fresh room. The door was open and no one else then Veronica, stood in midst of the door. Oh! No my heart screamed, Herbriella, change your place, but my mind drove me in fresh room to change myself and I got ready. Veronica has left the room before I came out, in fact no one was there waiting for me except Merletta. We locked the room behind and proceed towards the ground where we were supposed to go.

The ground in the mid of eight buildings was echoing Mrs. Brook's voice. We just slide through the crowd and found the place behind our seniors. Owing to Merletta's height, we passed until the first row. Mrs. Brook was looking excited. She was actively explaining about the spot we were going to visit today. Suddenly, I felt something heavy in my heart seeing Mrs. Brook... like I evoked I missed her all these days and the stream of emotions, which was graved in my heart wished to rush out. After she finished Mrs. Sailee asked us to form a queue to get into the buses waiting outside. But I could not ignore my feelings and ... went near Mrs. Brook and stared her... even she gazed me... it was the care... that her eyes sparked. But the next moment someone pushed me and I was able to hide my wet eyes.

"What's the matter Herbriella?" she asked holding me. I became speechless... thought once to tell her everything and ask her about my Mum's letter in turn... but then my eyes fell on George being humiliated by his friends and that instant thought vanished from my mind.

"I think you need... okay... Dr. Teasel... Dr. Teasel..." she beckoned Dr. Teasel who had already carried Merletta to look after.

"Rose, I think Herbriella needs you, hope you don't mind?"

"Oh not at all." And I was accompanied by Dr.Teasel and Merletta.

"Dr.Teasel, if you don't mind, can I call my friends with me." I asked her and knew she won't deny.

"Sure." I called my chums standing in a queue and even George without whom I cannot think to move on the earth.

All the four buses were packed and we were left to adjust in private van. My eyes fell on the tree house when we came to the end of the lane. Nevertheless, this wasn't a shock to me that a giant tree replaced the house we had once stayed in. I showed this to George and even to my chums and proved myself. As we turned to get into the van, we came across that gorgeous gate again. I remained last to get in on purpose to cram the beauty of gate properly. It yet looked opened and inclined me to get in.

"Herbriella." Dr. Teasel frisson me and I was already in the car at the window seat.

"Are you okay?" asked Nanisha. I threw a last look on the gate when car's engine came to life and followed the other buses.

We might have passed away many farms and huts, but I realized only when we came about the familiar vast scope on which several tents were built up. I told my chums that, George and I had been here before. This was the place where we met that weird woman, on which Dr. Teasel turned her head, "What did you say?" she asked.

"Nothing, I just guessed this place might be the victim." I shot into the dark.

"You are right; this is village 'Bunnie'. It is 15 kilometers far from Bhuj and 20 kilometers from our Dharamshala. It is among the most affected area and since then not able to rebuild."

"Why Ma'am?" Mouzami asked.

"Extreme poverty is the reason, anyhow they try to meet their ends but could not make up for loses they incurred."

All of us were asked to get out of the van once we reached there. It was difficult to guess the spread of tents beyond the edge of our sight. It was more than the vast area. People had no concern with our arrival; it was like a routine chore for them.

"People here are working hard to earn their livelihood. Many arts, skills they own and use the same to balance their life, hardly." Dr. Teasel said.

We all were divided into groups of fifteen-twenty students with one teacher for each.

Mrs. Brook asked everyone to stop as soon as we walked deep. "Choose your tent and collect as much information as you can. The subjects are same as yesterdays."

Our football team again paired up having Nanisha and Mouzami in addition. The rows at the front was taken by our seniors, searching the available we reached until the end and came to the row where half of the people were snoring on their 'Khat' [sack thread bed weaved on four legs of wood] We subdivided into small groups to interpret in detail. My chums, George and his two friends with me, approached a woman outside the tent who was sewing something.

"Good Morning…a…Miss…" she did not respond Bill.

"Bill, I think you should try in Hindi." George suggested.

"Right, okay…aye ladki tum kya karti ho? [Hey, girl what r u doing?]" Bill tried whatever he knew but we were sure to…

That woman just got up and said something angrily in Kutchi - a native language, moving towards Bill. First Bill was surprised, then feared of her and quickly buried himself behind us- three girls.

"Okay, so even you need the girls rally round?" George said sharply squinting at Rustin and I got him. I was just unable to control my laugh when George turned to me.

I tried softly in Hindi. I told her the reason for what we are here and I asked if she would like to help us. She calmed down and showed wonder with her big beautiful eyes. She was young and wore pink petticoat and maroon colored blouse which is known as Ghaghara and choli- a traditional Kutchi outfit. She suddenly raised her hand and pointed in right towards the tent.

I went ahead slowly followed by my companions. As we entered the tent, the scent of flowers gave me a familiar feeling. A space inside was neither dark nor bright with only one bulb illuminating in the corner far opposite. Many artifacts or say many weird things were displayed hanging or lying in the corner. It included artificial frog, tortoise, metal bells, crystals, etc. I guess the one breathing here must be involved in this weird business.

"I told you, you will come back." The voice behind the curtains quivered us. In the shade of the dim light, we saw the female figure stood in the midst of the raised curtain or the second door. When she came under the bright shade of light, I recognized her immediately. She was the same we came across while riding a camel- a Indo- American woman and I remembered her words too.

"How did you know..."

"You will come here right." She finished my sentence. "Well, you can count on me, if you believe Guruji." Her last word made her vital.

"Guruji? Who's this, when did you met them all?" Rustin asked and reminded me they were odd man.

"Oh nothing, it's all about Akka you remember, Mrs. Brook and I had the talk about." George tried to convince them.

"Okay but, who is this eerie lady and what is she talking about?" Bill proved himself smarter than Rustin did. It was now difficult to explain them, though I thank God for giving me best chums.

"Child, Guruji is the great holy preacher and I am his devotee and as Akka was also his devotee, we knew each other." Finding us in the hot water, that woman has to handle such muggles…oh the right word for the people not knowing and believing my real stories.

"A…Bill…Rustin… let the girls manage here, as though I am cheesed off these girly talks." Saying George dragged both of his stupid friends and irritated me for leaving me alone.

"Smart boy, Herbriella you have the right choice." That woman said.

"I am sorry, but he is my best friend…Miss…" she irate me even more.

"Kalindi…that's my Indian name and I would prefer you to call me with the same." She said raising her hand towards me and as I gave her mine, she pulled me towards her as though we came ear to ear. "Listen, concentrate on whatever Guruji has given you, it's very important." Automatically my eyes fell on my chums… but they were not aware… busy observing the articles. "I think you must leave now." She ordered me silently. I wished to be there some more time…but …okay. As I turned and moved, I slipped while saving my leg ready to step on the tortoise that might gets hurt. All the things I carried fell down to multiply my probs. Kalindi and later my chums helped me to gather the papers that flew out of my project file, all the stationery things that came out from compass box and my pet kit. Suddenly Kalindi laughed holding that tortoise upright. "You fell for this…it is artificial… doesn't look no? I have charged him with special powers."

"Powers?" all the three of us yelled.

"Oops, I shouldn't have said this." "Herbriella, it's yours, takes it."

"Why, what's the use?" I can never deny such unique gifts but Kalindi was smart to spill her beans.

"Everything in this world has some use, now or later."

"Hey, have you finished?" George looked eager. I bade good-bye to Kalindi and swiftly put that tortoise in my pet kit to walk with my companions.

Mrs. Rao announced lunch break arranging the venue in flat surface near the tents. Our food item was brought from the Dharamshala itself, then too, the natives there offered us their native dishes like Bhakari [bread], Undhiyu [vegetable], only Onion and Chilly for salad and Buttermilk. All of us waited for the signal to leap on at once. Nanisha and George started without bothering for anyone. I tried the native dish first; it was fun to eat such an original food. Moreover, more fun to drink tasty cool buttermilk that is also famous as 'Kutchi bear'. After having such a heavy lunch, one would definitely feel lazy. Our further step was not to walk anywhere but to rest for sometime in the shade of thick Peepal trees and cool Neem trees. We helped to spread out the mats on the rough muddy ground. Teachers and all elders helped themselves on Khat given by some natives. Our group found a place far from teachers taking care not to stay near Veronica and Lial as well.]

"Friends, rest for an hour and then we are going to have the fun." Mr. Newman said.

['Fun' we were going to have according to them, but the 'Rest' for most of us means to have a fun in our style.]

It is cool to live through the gift of nature, resting in the midst of greenery and feeling the warm and fresh wind being flippant around us… like… whooooooo. It is fun to have no stress, no mess…it is fun to be with friends… and of course, to play pranks.

Ethan- a ninth class guy, got up, swing on the branches of a giant tree, and was punished to disturb the calm nature… he fall down, made all laugh. To add in more entertainment Umang- a seventh class nut hit the Neem tree with the stone that was shading all our teachers. Those trees in turn started dropping down several green seeds of Neem and were enough to disturb out teachers and sirs. All at once got up and began to hunt for the cause behind this seeds downpour. The pupils who were spectators were unable to hide their teeth gave the hint and with Umang even they were punished to sit like a cock until the break time is over. This became fun for all, even for me but for a while.

[Suddenly I became uneasy …something was there diverting my mind… was it Veronica? No…then my letter with Mrs. Brook…not now… Kalindi… well, don't think so…then… I closed my eyes and … flash…saw the flashing opened door of the gate in front of our Dharamshala… instantly I opened my eyes.] The sight in front of me was sleepy, most of the pupils tired of their silly pranks were drawn to sleep and the teachers too …but I didn't see Mrs. Brook anywhere … not even Veronica and Lial… Oh, yes perhaps busy preparing other delicious cuisine for me. Merletta was sound slept with Dr. Teasel on her Khat. All a sudden, a creepy feeling raised my hairs and I lifted my head to check the buses on the edge of the road… if anyone's there…and really found someone's figure in the bus which faced in front of the tents we had visited… with this a tremendous scream of a woman thrilled everyone there. The noises attracted somewhere near the tent of Kalindi and I went into pieces. All at once got up to figure out, some of the natives ran towards the tent. Now the scream followed by the quaking of the bird and the people stepped rearward. No one dared to go there except one who just now

scurried from my side almost running further. It was Mrs. Brook. I guess she rushed from the direction I was spying. Her forward steps persuade others to follow. All of them together headed further. The screaming and quaking went on until the whole flock gathered around the tent. So my doubt was true, it was Kalindi's tent, the scene inside the rugs came to blows, it seemed. All the people outside were sizzling on every move of the wrestlers inside. Next moment we were jolted with the sudden fall of Mr. Newman. It seemed he was pushed down by something that vigorously hurried from the battle. The students who were nearer to Mr. Newman got back with the extreme howl. Teachers and few pupils including me tore the crowd somehow and saw Mr. Newman lying on the ground, trying to believe the thing that hit him was not real. However, the thing coiling and twirling was not his delusion. It was a real snake trying somehow to subsist, but the quaking followed by a huge, colorful Peacock snatched whatever his last breathe, smashing him finally.

"Hey, this is not done, you can't do this...hey... stop this." Mr. Apte shouted on Peacock.

"Shrikant, don't panic its the law of nature." Dr. Teasel said.

"Where did it go?" yelled Pranil. All of them turned where he referred and found no sign of snake or its carcass. The pride of Peacock was on its peak.

"This isn't the law of nature, I think." Said Ethan and we all were tensed.

"Yes, you are right, this isn't." the familiar voice came from the tent and Kalindi after saying this fell unconscious..."Oops" and before she knocks down Mr. Newman seized her.

"Oh, I know this woman." Rustin shouted as if he has gained his memory back right now.

"How?" asked almost everyone. Meantime, Mr. Newman carried

Kalindi into her tent.

"We met her to collect details for our project, but."

"But what? She didn't give?" asked Mrs. Sailee. I closed my eyes before Rustin opens his mouth again.

"No, she said something to Herbriella about Akka, and then we left them and approached another tent." All the eyes fell on me as I guessed.

"Anyway, let's not stretch this and you all should leave now." Mrs. Brook did not consider what Rustin told, Oh thank God!

"But Ma'am, we were going to visit other places." Aditi Sen- a ninth class girl said.

"Right, but we can't leave this woman here alone."

"So we have to stay here?" asked Amanda.

"No, Dr. Teasel and I will accompany Mr. Newman, the wards and rest all teachers will go back to Dharamshala." Mrs. Brook finally decided. [Oh no, I hope to stay here.]

"Only… You and your friends will be here." She said pointing towards me. She is just like my Mum, fulfilling my all desires O Wow! but that means she considered Rustin, Oh No again.

"Why Ma'am, even we want to stay here." Said Bill and got slap from Rustin. Mrs. Brook asked them to go in buses and leave the van for us. They all left but the natives surrounded us yet.

For the few moments, Mrs. Brook and Dr. Teasel investigated three of us. [Then I realized my chums were not aware of the talks I had with Kalindi, was my conversation secret? I guess.] Well again, I have to hide a lot from them when they believe me. I told them whatever Kalindi faked to Rustin and Bill. Both the Ma'am went to Kalindi's tent and asked us to remain out.

"Herbriea isn't it strange that none of her neighbor came to see her," asked Mouzami.

"Yes it's strange." Even Nanisha agreed. That means I am so keen on the matter inside that I did not realized this. Anyway, it is none of our business. Sometime later, our teachers came back and we followed them towards van. Therefore, we did not get the chance to see Kalindi for at least once. I saw the Peacock near Kalindi's tent, he looked most proud as though finished the significant task, and we moved towards Dharamshala, to the end of tragedies.

This was the terrible experience for all, so instead of pranks and jokes the serious murmuring was heard as we entered inside the Dharamshala. Everyone knew it was law of nature. The reptiles had to hide from these mighty birds. Nevertheless, the discussion was on the snake's disappearing, when all had seen the Peacock moving out from there after he has finished the snake. Therefore, even scholarly like Vishnu, Vidhya, Tierra and many such logs on to solve this riddle. Well, my eyes log on to search George and I found him; he was chatting with his friends and even checking up the main gate and saw me too. We all directly went to our rooms after having a dinner and without squandering on anything my roommates went to sleep, but I remained up, one of my roommates was missing in her bed- Veronica. After half-n hour, she got in slowly, taking the utmost care not to disturb us, but I was like disturbed with her every interference in my life itself. I saw clearly, she had carried something heavy in her hand and trying to place it in the space below the cupboard. She turned towards me and Instantly I closed my eyes.

It was not so bright day or it was the affect of the yesterday's incident, perhaps. Very first, I checked beneath the cupboard as I got the chance but found nothing. Even this time she was proved smarter than I. I was the last to step down.

Almost all the pupils and teachers were ready to enjoy holiday fun. Mrs. Brook had declared today no visit to victim areas. She was too much caring person.

First, I thought to remain in the Dharamshala and work on the Palace we have to search, but then it was impossible for Mrs. Brook to believe my excuses for us. Secondly, George insisted me to remain with others and not to leave any chance for our replicas to replace us again. Then even I thought it would be helpful for me to search for the Palace if it lies in our way. I again join with my friends and sat in the bus this time. First picnic point was the famous mountain of Bhuj, called 'Bhujiyo Dungar'. The lonely narrow road adjacent to the peak was the start to climb steps up.

"Wards who do not wish or not able to climb up, please remain in the bus itself." Mr. Apte said. Fatty Nattu of class eight willingly remain in the bus. Even Merletta was not allowed and for them Mrs. Rao and the helpers stayed down. Rests all jestingly proceed.

"There's a mythological story about this place, right?" I asked Dina, who had keen interest in the myth. She has read almost all the myth about India which she believes. "Yes, the place we are climbing is not the only mountain. It was a fort centuries ago and ruled by the King Bhujiyo, so it was named after him. The myth about it is that the King had slaughter the slithers who tried to end the human's breed in this village. The King burnt every reptile putting them under earth and calmly left the fort forever. Nevertheless, the myth about the snake is that they came back for their revenge. They finished off the King when he turned up again in the fort on new moon night. Therefore, it is believed that the snakes come out especially on every new moon night and hence it is banned to come here for 15 days including Amavasya that is New Moon night." This was dangerous. Everyone silently listened her and hesitate to proceed.

"Dina, do not scare them." Dr. Teasel scolded her. "All these are fables; we should not take this in." However, Dr. Teasel tries, wards had already taken in, since they have come to sense. Elders always deny it as real and we children die out to prove it. Some day some may we succeed and that could be I.

Dina's story gave a boost to our passion to move faster. Within half-an hour, we climbed up, and then walked the long alley with the huge brick walls both the sides. Finally, we came in front of the huge old fort as though we have shuffle in history. At the end of the long passage, the vast surrounding of the fort started. With huge pillars, the main entrance lied closed and we had to take pleasure of the outer contiguous only.

"Bad luck, it is closed." Mr. Apte said. Even then we tried from each side of the fort, might we find any secret entry and instead found many crusts of the snakes. So it was not the myth, it was real and this added to our interest. All of them picked up the peels and I started finding the match for the one I had in my pocket. I took out my belonging. "Sh... what are you doing?" asked George from behind, watching my every movement.

"George, if I find the match, then this is the spot we are looking for." I said excitedly.

"But it is not a Palace."

"That could be fort as well; it was ruled by the King. And according to Dina's story, it gives us hint, I guess."

"No, I don't think so." Mouzami said.

"Let's see." George winded up on others arrival.

"Come on wards, come back." Mrs. Rienzi shouted on the few students trying to climb up the pillars as well. We were asked to go down fast.

"George, shall we tell Mrs. Brook about this, otherwise we will have to go back." I suggested.

"No we can't. She will never believe us."

"But then we will make her believe." I insisted.

"No use, we have no proofs." Mouzami said.

"I have some, and we can even take them to Kalindi again, she will definitely help us."

"Kalindi? Who said this?" asked Mrs. Brook and we all moved down silently. Further George convinced me about the possibility of havoc, if Mrs. Brook gets us wrong.

"How can you say, this cloth is the proof?" asked Mouzami.

"I feel, this is the root and will take us to the place I need to go." I was truly certain about it.

"So what next?" Nanisha asked assuring their prop.

"We will come back, if necessary." I said.

Moreover, we all headed towards our next spot- 'Aaina Mahal'.

It was the Museum of Mirrors, representing us differently. Our tiredness of fruitless trekking on 'Bhujiyo Dungar' disappeared as we entered Aaina Mahal. In a moment, the museum turned into the amusement hall.

 "Oh, I got my figure back, wow!" shouted Bhoomi of class ninth standing in front of the bony mirror. Nattu tried the same mirror and bowling he covered his face. "What? Even you got your figure?" Pranil teased him, when he too tried to see his physic and the shock widen his eyes to bulge out. Few more students wished but could not dare; instead, out of her curiosity Mouzami dragged us to see the matter. We burst out of laughter to see Nattu doubled his size in mirror and Pranil lost all his muscles leaving the bones like a skeleton. Therefore, this was the reason of their funny faces. Oh Jesus, it was amazing, an array of Mirrors made up our day. If anyone is on trip to Bhuj, I will strongly recommend this- the must place to visit. Deepali wanted to have a Zero figure and she got. Nattu always worried for his obesity and he too got more. Pranil is keen for his muscles to come out and they went out totally. Hey, this was the Mirror of 'wish and the same Mirror that Harry had found; let me check. I stood in front of the mirror and wished to see the Palace... no response. I changed my mind and wished to see something touchy- my Mum. "Herbriella, what are you doing here? Come out fast." interrupted Mrs. Brook and went away. I found none of my friends with me, not even George. Now I must go, but let me take the last chance. This time I wished to see the thing, person, or anybody that is chasing me. "So you are hiding here, dunce." It was Veronica to alarm me. "We are not at your service to treat you special, come fast." I missed my last chance too. I wonder, in fact, I remember now, the Veronica and Lial's absentee on the mountain. Well, it is his entire wish, after all.

My friends could not hold their laughs even at the halt, where we stopped to have our lunch. The place was like typical, mainly seen on the highways and was called 'Dhaba'. Spread out in vast space with the sand all around with the few bushes dried out. We willingly had Kutchi dish of Bhakari and Brinjal for vegetable. The owners were very kind to allow us stay over throughout the burning noon. I said everything to George and my chums during our rest time. They now did not question me.

After two hours of the rest, we headed towards the coolest spot of Bhuj-Hamirsa Lake. Nevertheless, the lake dried out due to the scanty rainfall in entire Kutch. However, the natives say it a fabulous feeling when they have enough of rainfall. Really, in spite of dryness, the wind showered its coolness on us.

"Okay, wards we are now going to Market, and you all are allowed to shop..." before Mrs. Sailee can complete all the nuts shouted, including me.

"Wait let me finish. You can shop only that is relevant things and with our permission only. Is that clear?" Yet we all cheered up and became wild to reach there as early as possible.

I had been always attracted towards the ancient traditional Antiques. Therefore, I decided not to miss this excellent opportunity. It took half-n hour to reach the market place. The various, colorful stalls welcomed us from a long distance. The systematic display of all the stalls was heart taking. First, the attire stall displayed the embedded Kutchi traditional dresses of all the varieties. We liked it, but had no use so we moved further. In similar get up the varieties of home décor was like ready to dress up your home traditionally. I stopped there to ask the sort of materials used in it. It was called 'Toran'- festoon like that people tie on their door pane, during festivals and occasions. The materials used in it were small mirror- abhala, golden threads- tui jari, etc. and were used to decorate the lamps, wall hangings and lot more. We were allowed to buy anything with permission. But the thing of my choice had not yet appeared. George found it useless, so he moved towards the games and rides further. Mouzami and Nanisha stuck to the stall of colorful traditional accessories and I remained in the midst to find out my choice. Then my eyes fell on the number of stalls arranged at the end exhibiting an ancient currency of Kutch, various Taveez, few alike to one George had tied, an ancient big stones, gems, metal bells, different stone accessories and lot more and the familiar faces of the people I had seen near Kalindi's tent. They were the same neighbors' about whom Mouzami had commented. Oh God, I think I will find out Kalindi. I ran the whole alley with the stalls both the sides and checked them, but Kalindi was nowhere. I was fraught to find no sign of her, whereas all the Bunnie natives were here. Even she had the same work, and then she ought to be here. What should I do? Should I call my friends to my help? Oh, it will take time. No, I must search for her myself. I approached an old woman vendor to ask about Kalindi. "Who is this Kalindi? I don't know her.," that woman said. It was strange.

"Yesterday she had an encounter with snake and the Peacock came to her rescue, don't you remember, aunty." It was difficult to explain her in Hindi.

"Yes, I saw the snake and the Peacock, but there was no woman involved." She gave me the great shock. "And for the last ten years I am living here, I had never seen or heard about the woman you are describing." Even she looked surprised. Well, I tried few more people and got the same answer from them. It was not my illusion and that could be proved with the help of not one or two but the entire Minerva secondary students and the teachers. I ran fast to tell my friends about this shocking news, but then I lost my way and remained confused among the tremendous crowd towards the opposite. Frustrations enfold me as I thought about Kalindi. Who was she? How she knew Guruji? Did he send her? Then why she disappeared? I graved into darkness, in spite of flashlights focusing strongly.

Tire out of my tries, I looked out of the market place where our buses were parked and resolved to go there. Shouting vendors and bargaining buyers did not compel me to stop, and I easily reached there. I found my bus and was about to step up when I heard the familiar voice.

"Okay, you have done the good job." I knew something is cooked up. It was Veronica.

"We didn't get her." Obviously, it was Lial.

"Never mind, better luck next time," said Veronica.

"When?" Asked Lial.

"Tonight, it's going to be the…" and she left the sentence. I was like burning on fire; I cannot wait for the deadly night to fall. I must go to Mrs. Brook. That is the final thing remaining yet to do. As I turned to go, George seized me. "Are you crazy?"

"No today you can't stop me."

"Herbriea, calm down please."

"You say this as you don't know the thing I have heard and for that I have to go to Mrs. Brook now… at least."

"I know for what you are so desperate. I saw you were running randomly and I followed you and heard the same you have."

"Then yet you need me to keep mum."

"Tell me if you had any solid proofs to convince Mrs. Brook." George was annoyed. "Look Herbriea, nothing is gained by haste and anger. Unless, we have enough evidence no one will believe us, so please calm down." He sounds like Dr. Teasel right now. This much counseling was enough to cool me.

"George, I know something more than you." Then I told him about Kalindi. He too was shocked and asked me to think deeply about what Guruji has insisted me.

We stopped conversing as soon as our companions dawdle out after enjoying the entire shopping. Within half-n hour, we were carried to Dharamshala. Mrs. Brook called us in dining hall after getting freshen up, so we moved towards our room.

Vijay Vilas Palace

As we were asked, we moved towards our room though, I did not wish to face Veronica again. She was the damn brave to stay with her victim. Once I thought to ask on her face about her talk with Lial, but I had to purse my lips on George's intend.

When we gathered in the dining hall, George and my chums suggest me the remedy to change the place.

"You can ask Mrs. Brook for this." Nanisha tried her head.

"No way, she will ask me to clear my breast with Veronica as she didn't know the cause."

"You are right, so then what can we do?" agreed Mouzami.

"I have an idea, if you wish..." said George frantically.

"Yes, all of you pay attention. Gather in the ground at once." Mr. Newman said this as we finished our dinner. George told me to share his brain on the ground. All were excited to get there. The students chose their group. Playing games was not compulsory so we sat on the fence around the Peepal tree. Among the entire Minerva people, I found out Veronica sitting under the tree far in the corner, aloof with Lial... so they were planning for tonight... she had the good chance for what she needed.

"George, what are you waiting for, c'mon tell us." I tick off him for lavishly watching the football match played on the ground.

"Oh sorry! Okay look if Veronica is involved in all this..."

"What do you mean by 'If'?" I yelled at him.

"Okay, believe she is involved, and then she definitely knows our replicas, right?"

"So what?"

"So you can stay at least one night with her, if ...if... she believes you as your replica." George said.

"But how?" all three of us asked together.

"Simple... pretend as you are her best friend as you was in train."

"Duffer... she doesn't know we were replaced and because of Mrs. Brook she shared with us."

"That's what she pretends in open, but she knows the truth."

"What truth?" asked my chums and I told them about the market incident.

"I told you so, something is strange about Kalindi. Did you see none of her neighbor took effort to see her?" Mouzami reminded.

"I am worried about her. According to Veronica and Lial, they were aiming to get someone tonight and that could be Kalindi, I guess." I expressed my doubt.

"But you said she is already missing." Mouzami asked.

"That means tonight..." Nanisha's eye fixed on me.

[The cool night suddenly became warm and the trees around turned vigorous, small bushes beside the trees went wild and passed the wind forcibly. It was a simple change of nature for some... but dire for... Herbriella and... for Veronica... she smiled fiercely.]

"Come on friends... it's time to go now." Said Mr. Newman until now playing football with the students accompanied by Apte sir.

We moved tiredly towards our quarter and said good night to one another. [Maybe for the last time]. All my roommates' were quiet under the cloak of dark, even Veronica. Thank God, she saved me from playing her good friend role. I took out my pet kit from coat and lit up tiny lighthouse to check my bedding. Merletta slept soundly beside my bed. Finally, I lied down, closed my eyes but kept my ears open if any important movement I come by. With my closed eyes, I put the torch back in the kit and ouch... got a sharp cut on my little finger. I again ensure the things in my pouch and found one conical shaped thing. I saw it properly in the torch light; it was a bud... a flower bud. I do not remember how it came into my kit or when did I picked it, whatever I was feeling sleepy right now. Therefore, that thing has to go back in its place.

[Veronica got up as Herbriella shut her eyes. She took out the thing she had hidden beneath the cupboard and placed it near the window. She moved her hands around the thing as if hexing it secretly. The light flashed awhile later and the antique petal shape box came to life.]

"Oh I am late... too late." Suddenly I got a jerk. The rays it seemed illuminated the room... but it had the black tinge behind. I could hear my roommates' snore, however before I could rouse them; I went near the window and what's this? It wasn't day fall yet... then...how is this place so glowing? I went back to my bed and checked the time in my wristwatch. It showed quarter to three. Then this was the flash and not the rays of the sun... I again went to the window, opened the glasses and strained to see from where it beamed and got it... yes it was from... a Gorgeous Royale Gate... inside which I missed to enter...I decided... no one else was awake... shall I call George ...at this hour?...no way. So it's done... again I moved my hand to find out my torch and felt Merletta was not in her bed... was neither any flash...nor the window was open. ...

Oh! This nightmare, the time was half past five, early on; I crumple to lie down on my bed and stir back at once...MERLETTA - OH NO! She was truly not in her bed and I got freeze. Only I was up to search for her. She was neither in the fresh room, nor in the possible corners. Without disturbing my room-mates [especially Veronica] I checked the room to see any other door it had and found the main door opened. Oh no! Once I saw the sleeping girls, I pulled in the door and shut down slowly after getting out. After all, it wasn't a leisure time for me, so it was wise to climb down like a cat. I headed towards... I didn't know where.

[Once Herbriella went down, Veronica got up from her bed again and

So what on the earth attracted Merletta to go out of the main gate, what
was on her mind? I don't know why but I feel Merletta has definitely
entered the Royale Gorgeous Gate.

Out the surrounding was darkest and the bushy part looked like the
ghosts staring me and spreading their hands to reach me. Only the door
looked alive. It was flashing and attracting. Just for Merletta I decided to
go in. The door went open as I stood in front of it. No one was guarding
there. I ensured around if anyone's chasing.

As soon as I stepped in the bright rays tore out the dark shroud of
night… the leaves pop out to live out greenery… the baby birds just got
their tongue to chirp in gay… the sweet honey overflow with every hum
of the bees… the bushes stretched themselves in a salute to welcome
someone special and … the bunches of flowers bloomed to enhance the
orchard, yes, that similar orchard I have come by many times in my
dreams. A fresh, caring and thrilled breeze wrapped me, as I walked
through the orchard on the red carpet onto which the flowers pour down
at my each step ahead. I was absorbed in the beauty of nature and
wished to freeze this forever. Moreover, will not mind where this
orchard leads me, I just want to live this to my content.

*[Herbriella, though the part of this life, had to prove her ability…ability to
face whatever… to fight whatever… and to find and reach her destiny,
whatever efforts it demands to save it from the forthcoming danger. The
deadly creature, who turn up to finish his incomplete deed since century;*

crawled in the upper layer of the soil along with the roots of the thorny bushes and moved behind Herbriella, gradually getting nearer. It looked not less than Ogre - a Slithering Ogre.]

Orchard with thick bushes and beautiful flowers end at the sight of beautiful, wonderful, Gorgeous, huge Palace, and WOW! MY DREAM PALACE. Same Palace built in pinkish brown marble stones, with several windows, same motifs, but no words, which I had mused. The Palace was surrounded by the royal garden both the sides and the way of orchard led me to the entrance of it. Same dull crafty door with several tiny square sections borne by the bells ringing together. Suddenly my eyes fell on the human figure stood in the middle of the royal stairway. An old man dressed in traditional outfit [Dhoti and Vest] holding a wooden stick for support was a guard it seemed.

Elders say do not waste your time worrying on what you do not have. Right, well saying, yet I wasted my time regretting on not asking Harry to lend me his invisible cloak. Without which I will have to face that old man, anyhow I proceed. His eyes fell on me as I climb few steps upward. I tried to explain him about my need to come here, but he did not respond and went on digging his ears, until then I entered the main door. I do not remember I had seen a big spacious lounge at first that resembled to the King's courtroom, usually read or seen in the stories. It was furnished with the several royal chairs for the courtiers arranged in two rows facing opposite to one another. At the end of the rows, lie the King's thrones adorned with various gemstones. Nobody seemed to be present right now from any of the King's descendants, so it looked secluded, yet gorgeous. The King's royal seat fascinated me to feel the touch. Gradually my hand moved further, when a sudden shriek hinders me to continue. [*Herbriella could not see the tiny slithers resting behind the throne came to life and before they could loop out, she turned away.]* Obviously, the noise came from the throne itself. With this, the flight of butterflies encircled me for a while and then move about in the rift to the left, tempting me to pursue. They led me into the bright lobby with full of arcane. The effigy of guards with swords was sited at every four- five feet distance resting beside the sidewall. Should I go ahead? A question arose to me. Merletta's innocent face appeared on my dark eyelids and I resolved. Suddenly the footfalls from behind trigger me to hide somewhere. Finding no hiding place, I ran behind one of the statue. This gave me the chance to touch it. I peeped through the gap between the statue's elbow and saw... oh thank God. "George!" I screamed mutely.

"Herbriella? Jesus! You are crazy." He was panting. I stretched my lips and rolled my eyes around the place we stood and lifted my nose to show the pride. George followed whatever I expressed and...

"After all you found out your dream Palace." he got me.

"Yes, at last." I said frantically.

"But, you shouldn't have come alone."

"I know, I decided to call you but Merletta gave me no chance."

"Merletta?" He frowned with a shock.

"Yes she is here and I am here to take her back."

"Oh no, let's find her before anyone else can caught us." George dragged me to the left staircase and we came across another lobby at the end of the steps.

[Herbriella found out George chasing her, but they together were unaware of one more shadow chasing them.]

The third lobby led us to the legroom both the sides, but locked.

[History repeats its own. The sight outside the Palace was the same as it was outside the Castle, century ago. Number of bushes increased including the thick trees along with their roots and concealed the Palace encompassing. The birds stopped singing and stayed calm to buoy up. Butterflies left their bit and found the place closest to Palace. It looked like the earthly Doomsday following. The weird creatures swaying in the air

proved that the deed will be definitely ended this time at any cost... at what cost?]

It was as if we were in the ship now, but no matter anything with George beside me. "George, you would have brought my chums together."

"They were not in their room. But I thought they might be with you." Passing away the lobby we came in front of the room, that was unlocked but the doors were closed. George slowly pushed the door and found the height of surprise. Mrs. Brook and Dr. Teasel were busy doing something. I pushed the door little harder and saw they were digging out something from the shelves and cupboards quickly. "George, don't stop me today." I said. We entered and shocked Dr. Teasel who was busy throwing out something from the royal, huge cupboards with the carved plates and the long mirror on its door. Mrs. Brook was trying the royal bed picking up the bedspreads and cushions. "Herbriella? George? Who gave you the permission?" Asked Dr. Teasel controlling herself and then Mrs. Brook noticed us. Both of them fade away to find unexpected. We kept quiet for a while.

"Ma'am, we are here for Merletta." I said confidently.

"Merletta? Why?" Both of them asked together.

"Why? Sorry but even you were not expected here? I thought..."

"Err yeah...right yeah we were...we were just looking for ... ugh..." Dr. Teasel stammered, "For Merletta." Mrs. Brook completed her sentence wiping her forehead. Dr. Teasel narrowed her eyes and Mrs. Brook gave her quick look. I knew they were on something else.

"Where in cupboard and under the bed?" George used his brains. Pin drop silence for a while.

"Uh...well, we will not hide anymore." Mrs. Brook broke the silence first coughing a little and gave the decisive look to Dr. Teasel.

"Today let me tell you the truth. We are here for your mother's letter, Herbriella." She raised my discontent desire.

"My Mum's letter... but you had already given me"

"Well, no, I kept one with me."

"Why Ma'am?"

"I thought it was too early to hand it to you." Mrs. Brook said wearily holding the letter.

I stared her.

"I didn't want you to be more disturb... so."

"Then why did you come here, Ma'am." George asked.

"It was my decision to arrange an educational trip to this place..."

"Was it so crucial?"

She glimpsed Dr. Teasel once, "Yes, as I wanted to solve the riddle behind..." and she scrupled a while "behind... your origin." I was dumbfounded to hear, beyond my brains.

"Take this; read it... after all it is yours." Without considering my reactions Mrs. Brook gave me the piece of paper, for me it was my Mum herself. I just grabbed and started reading it.

"My dearest Herbie, my only angel, my little magician, I know you adore magic and will rock the world with your magic tricks. My blessings are with you forever.

Herbie, before the truth of your life, I will tell you one story. The story starts ten years ago when I met Prince Virat Singh Jadeja in Vijay Vilas Palace; he was the last descendant. I was entrusted with the assignment on History of forts left aloof in Bhuj. You were not aware that initially I was an Archeologist and working for London Govt, as I never had told you. We fall in love, instantly were married and lived happily.

It was a rainy night, never expected. I set off home owing to unbearable labor pain. It was ready for due. However, that freaky night changed my entire life. That was the nightmare for me and the only reason for which I survived was you. Herbie, be strong and listen. That night I found an infant baby in the Palace. I could hardly snatch it from the evils and took with me,

forever. It was a baby girl... it was you. You are not my real daughter ..."
I paused for a while looking to Mrs. Brook and she admitted nodding.
This wounded me a lot. I continued reading, "and my Hus#######. *I
know you are shocked"* the scribble part seemed crucial but illegible so I
continued reading, "*Like you even I was alone in this entire world.
Therefore, I left my work as an Archeologist and took up a teaching job in
Canada. I decided to live a peaceful life with you, burying my bitter past.
First I thought you handle on magic tricks when you clear out household
mess in a while or when our neighbors appreciate your boundless strength
for lifting the weights at such early age and even when you once wished to
have wings and straight in front of me you got a colorful butterfly to rest
on the flower. It was the most amazing and unbelievable sight. Well, I have
always imagined you as a great magician. However it was awful to see you
howl in your bed or sometimes rushing into the wood in fear and suddenly
getting unknown to your weird behavior. None of the psychiatrics' detected
your complications but I knew what to do. Your weird dreams, strange
behavior compelled me to dig out your origin. Again, I brought you to
India, admitted you in Boarding school and lost my peace. I wandered days
and nights to find about you. However, my efforts did not pay me; I failed
to get you to your parents... biological parents. Now I am leaving you this
job to finish, Herbie. I know it is difficult to start only with the base of Gold
pendant..."* I again looked Mrs. Brook and she admitted. *"... tied in
your neck and the antique chest, when I found you. Yet, I know you can do
it. I have no spare time, but you can count on Mrs. Brook, she will help
you. So my little magician all the very best throughout your life and lots of
love and hopes, in some epoch we may be together to lead a happy long life.
Good-bye sweetie and take care..."* and the drops of my tears blotted the
words 'kisses'.
I remembered that very next day I was taken to her funeral, on fifth of
December. I was out of my words   and mind too.

"Herbriea, I am sorry." George said holding my shoulder.

"Herbriea, it's okay." Mrs. Brook consoled me taking me into her arms.

"Herbriea, be brave and accomplish your Mum's dream." Dr. Teasel reminded me of my deed and I just shed out my tears.

Mrs. Brook gave me that Gold Pendant. It was cute tiny leafy shape with vertical contour dividing two parts and as soon as I touched that, both the parts opened like a door and one more similar flap haul up rising up an oval chest. It enclosed fresh green shrubbery seeds.

"George, pinch me." I said this to believe incredible scrutiny. However, those people had not yet come around.

"Amazing!" said Dr. Teasel.

"Well, the thing knows its owner." Mrs. Brook committed. "Take out those seeds." She asked and I put them on my palm. Next few second we waited for another magic, however, nothing happened.

"Herbriea, you never said you knew this Palace." Mrs. Brook asked.

"I had seen it sometimes in my daydreams."

"You could have told us before." Dr. Teasel said.

"I thought you all won't believe me, But Ma'am, you had my letter since my Mum left me, then why did you waited so long."

"No, I got this letter just two days before your medical checkup and that was the reason to call you for tests."

"Then who gave you, Ma'am?"

"Your Mum had left this with her only friend in Canada and Mrs. Millie Reeves, your aunt send it to me along with the donations for your further studies."

"That means Mrs. Gold knew her disease from first." George guessed.

"Yes, she was suffering from Liver psoriasis that chases till one's end." Dr. Teasel said sadly.

"One more thing, Herbriea, all the Kathy's property has been transferred on your name."

"Oh!" though I was not her own blood, then to she loved me so much.

"Then what about her child, she said she was expecting that night." Dr. Teasel asked.

"Well, that night something had happened that changed her life." George added.

"What could have happened that night that she lost her baby and got me instead? And what about her husband-the Prince Virat Singh Jadeja or say my father?" I doubted.

"No, he couldn't be your father. We have even tried to figure out the scribbled portion in this letter and before coming here we searched for her husband through various sources, but found nothing. Not even the details regarding this Palace was available and so I decided to visit

"Yeah, Julianne is right. We have gone through minute information we come by." Dr. Teasel said.

"Ma'am, Prince Virat is the only key, live evidence on that night, only he can tell us what happened to my Mum, to their child and maybe about me." I became vigorous.

"You are right, Herbriella. But he is not with us right now or might..."

"Might he has passed away, too, err... in case." Dr. Teasel cut short Mrs. Brook which she didn't agree with. Mrs. Brook changed her deep sight towards the seeds I carried and I felt something fishy, anyway...

"All she mentioned about was this Palace; I think we must start from the beginning." she said and we all moved downward.

"Ma'am, what were you doing in that room?" George asked while getting down.

"As we climbed up we saw this room opened. So we just went through in hope to come around any clues." Dr.Teasel said.

I had carried those seeds down carefully. We started hunting in every nook and corner of the courtroom, but in vain. All of us gathered in the core after futile efforts when suddenly Mrs. Brook bend down and rubbed her hand on the carpet on the floor. Even we joined her. "Rose, don't you feel it's different?" She asked.

"No, it's the same, rough and tough. I had never liked this pattern." We all stared her yet she did not get us.

"Dear, I am talking about the bumpy surface; look it seems it has grown meadows on it." We again rubbed our hands against it and found according to Mrs. Brook.

"Herbriea spread out these seeds here." She said and I did. The second moment the tiny grass grew larger to touch the maximum and tow us in the world of thorny foliage. With this, the floor beneath us bust into cracks and came out a huge old crafty basin tapering up its nub beyond our reach with the tiny outlet. The dull brown twigs everywhere replaced the royal furnishings. We went aside and clasped our hands with each other's. "Ma'am, there's something wrapped around the nub." George drew our attention towards it, and I leapt to get that. Once I went inside the basin climbing its huge wall, its nub started spinning itself.

"Herbriea, come out fast." Mrs. Brook said and other two screamed. I too wished to get out soon but not without the thing. My guts insisted me to get the hold of the spinning nub, anyhow and I spring on it at once and grab the wrapped thing. It was an old parchment depicted something on it. I unfold it and found an ancient writing. Yet, the spinning did not cease. "Herbriea, read aloud." Mrs. Brook said as I again climbed out the basin.

"ITS GREEN, IT'S FRESH, READY TO STRETCH.

THOUGH COLD TO HOLD, IT'S THE WAY THROUGH THE BOWL." Half of it was already solved on George's face. "Yes?" he was asked.

"Look, its green that means Frog, its fresh means it lives in water and it has to jump to move so it stretches its body. That's it, so simple." He said taking all credit. I was impressed by his science knowledge.

"No, this doesn't go with the description. Think something else." Said Mrs. Brook and it was fun to watch George's grimace.

"Listen, its green and fresh means grass, tree, leaves anything related to it and ready to stretch means to grow up and they are cool to touch." Dr.Teasel seemed to solve the half of it.

"But its the way through the bowl…" and all of them stared me.

"MA'AM!" shouted George.

"What?"

"Ma'am Merletta; we did not find her."

"Have you both seen her coming here?"

"No."

"Then, how can you say she is here. Come on don't waste time and concentrate." Mrs. Brook was annoyed.

"I think we must get into the bowl and try there." I suggested.

"How can you say that, it's the bowl to be find and not the basin?" Dr.Teasel said.

"Herbriea is right, Rose. Imagine this basin to be smaller in size and then think." Mrs. Brook got me right but Dr.Teasel looked uneasy for not getting so simple thing. We all literally climbed in. It was quite copious to hold all of us together. We all tried from different sides of the inner wall by touching it, scratching it, rubbing it and George even tried to push it, but no signs.

"Okay anyone have the torch so that we can dig out something if it's hidden." Asked Mrs. Brook and I recalled my pet kit.

"Ma'am, I have nail shaper instead." I had the one but dimmed torch.

"Not bad, give it."

I took out my nail filer with other dozens of things and was hurt again by that rough bud.

"What's this?" asked Mrs. Brook looking at the fallen bud.

"It's a bud; I don't know from where I had." I said while picking it up and that was the moment that the bud swoop itself from green to glimmering gold. I came to my sense and without asking anyone I again jumped in the air and fixed that bud in the outlet of spinning nub. Within a second, the spinning was stopped and the bud stretch up to bloom the petals of flower that started pouring out the chilled water and… "Oh no Herbriea, what you did?" …George yelled at me. Nevertheless, the swirling inside the water was not helping. It was bashful to make my helpers suffer with me, but I was helpless. All of us tried hard to get out. Our slippery hands did not lend a hand to us to climb up and we slip down each time we tried. The water filled up to the rim. Obviously, we dived holding one another. The pour went on and we went on stirring.

"So it was about this cold water and now we are going to find out the way through it." Mrs. Brook said this hardly. I sighed out of relief. "What way?" asked Dr. Teasel.

While whirling into the chilled water I came across the words I have mused. Yes! I smashed the water. They were engraved on the crafty inner wall of the basin. Those Sanskrit words were unable to be read by my companions so were unnoticed. Totally drenched under the waterfall I was able to read only a single-single word of the canto. I found George trying to get closer. "What are you doing?" asked George could not shut his mouth, even in the chilled water. After finishing the whole verse once, I read it aloud.

"JALAM DEVAH, DADATI MARGAHA." And according to my sense it was a request to the God of water to lead us the way.

I repeated those words loudly breathing deep once, until the nub itself spin out from the midst and we all swift into the gap. The dark narrow gap did not allow us to think, yet I weigh up on the Sanskrit words I mused and found out the way.

"OOUCH…" this was the only reaction after getting on the rooty surface with dual force. Well, I did not guessed the way to be so rough.

"Miracle, not a single drop of water we have carried down." Dr. Teasel said without feeling her hairs in mishmash state, owing to the rooty tunnel I guess.

"Nothing is bizarre in Herbriea's reign." George said trying to hold his mirth as he sighted Dr. Teasel and I told him to ignore.

"Anyway, this smells to be the dungeon." Mrs. Brook said exploring the surrounding. "Herbriea, have you learned Sanskrit?" Suddenly she changed the topic.

"No Ma'am." I replied without facing her.

"Then how can you solve that verse?"

"I don't know, Ma'am. This is not the first time I had spoken such words but, that I don't remember now."

"I know you had used this language in Rose's clinic too. But I wonder how you can use when it is banned to speak within Minerva premises." She gave the information, which I knew.

"Why, Ma'am." George asked.

"The story is too long, two of the teachers were found dumb while teaching Sanskrit in the class and later they admitted that they were threatened prior not to use this language anywhere by anyone, yet they tried and paid." Mrs. Brook opened her mind whiles we were passing the dark lobby.

"But Ma'am we can use this language outside our premises." I asked her.

"That Mrs. Chaturvedi tried once and was extremely horrified that she didn't even dare to share her experience." Oh, that's why she yelled at me and was found tearing and burning all the Sanskrit books. Then how did Mr. Newman helped me? Oh no.

It was really a Rooty dungeon. It was full of roots entangled in one another. We were perplexed, as there was no further way.

"Come on Herbriea, say something in Sanskrit." George said.

"It comes on its own." Saying this I touched one root and the deathly howls and screams tore out our ears that coerce us to remain in the center. Suddenly the roots got closer towards us, and it seemed to dupe us. I had faced the similar mayhem, so I tried to recall those Sanskrit words I spoke at that time.

"Herbriea, we are in trouble." George said whacking the twigs that tried to entangle us together. I grew my instinct to crop up those words again. "Herbriea, do something." Trying to get rid of the shoot Dr. Teasel counted on me. In fact, I was their entire hope. I thought I was helpless, when some of the twigs bound us together tightly; I felt vibes and bellowed 'BHASKARA JWALAKAM.' Within no seconds, the rooty barriers went off and elevated, leading us in the enormous glimmering scope.

Chap- 18

Earthly Doomsday

"Look out!" I screamed, as the next step was to drag us in the chasm around us and we were fenced in. It looked similar to the hellhole and the fire might burst out anytime. The earth beneath us was not plain; it bears many splits and cracks.

"What is this Herbriea?" asked Dr. Teasel.

"Definitely we all are trapped." replied Mrs. Brook.

"So this was the plan." I mumbled.

"What plan?" asked Dr. Teasel.

"George, did you find Veronica in her place?" I asked.

"Err… well; yes … no actually I did not see her."

"Ma'am, Veronica promised to get someone and now she has done it." She got more than one.

"Yes Ma'am, she is right." George helped me.

The scope was glowing like the sun.

"Herbriea, I think it is the result of your spell." George said timidly.

"So you thought it is easy, right."

"Did you know its gist?"

"No, but I guess, 'come out of the one and get trap into the other'." I said this annoyingly.

"Calm down, Herbriea, don't lose your mind." Dr. Teasel said this slowly and moved little ahead, but was petrified and suddenly could not move. Mrs. Brook hurried to hold her and tried to make her sit. Instead, her whole body leaned down and remained like a stone.

"Ma'am, it's all because of me." I said unable to control my tears.

"Don't cry and try to find out how it happened."

"Look Herbriea, something is carved on the earth." said George showing me uneven lines that were engraved on the earth on which we stood. Yes, those lines looked specific and I thought the earth was damaged.

"No George, don't touch them." Mrs. Brook screamed as soon as George tried to get close to it. I remembered Guruji's metal sheet that I possess now and he had asked me to follow my soul. I checked with mine, which were very important according to Kalindi as well. George started repeating the mantra that Guruji had given him. I closed my eyes to get any signal and…

"Herbriea, touch them." Mrs. Brook asked me as she glance the metal sheet. I got my answer. I sat down and touched all the lines one by one. Nothing happened to me, but the lines on the earth curved and formed into circle and another lines set themselves to shape into the sign of 'Sun'. As soon as I touched the sign of sun, it split open and threw all of us aside with bursting out the dry something from beneath. It was huge and looked liked a flower, a colorless flower or an old antique of it. It had the seven petals with lifeless brown tinge, and had the part of the scalene stone in one of its petal. I notched out the piece and matched it with the scalene stones I had.

"It is the right one." George said.

"Yes and the last one." The shape of the petal formed as I kept that last part correctly, but the parts did not join.

"Herbriea, I think it will need a special spell." Dr. Teasel said. I was happy to find her fit again. "I felt some burning light entering my body and flew out as I opened my eyes." She said interestingly. In spite of being the quarry once, she was enjoying.

"Ma'am, I am happy to have you safe." We watched the petal feebly. No one spoke as the minds were on how to join the petal.

"You can do it, Helbliella." Again it was a pleasant surprise. Thunder roars were audible to us even though we were graved.

[The nature was fret on the future encounter between the Good and Evil. The evil thorny roots gathered around the Palace, found the way in.]

Merletta stood at the other side of the Hellhole was afraid to get into the chasm.

"Oh Merletta, how did you came here?" asked Mrs. Brook.

"We searched for you all over." George said.

"But why have you come here?" Dr. Teasel asked.

"Merletta, its dangerous, do not step ahead." I said.

"Yes, but not fol me." She said bravely.

"That's okay, but you should have told me at least." I said caringly.

"Were you lost?" asked Mrs. Brook.

"No, Ma'am I am on the light path, if you give me that I can join it fol you, Helbliea." She traumatized us entirely. We were speechless.

"Don't waste the time Helbliea." Suddenly her voice raised and seemed to order me.

"But how did you know..."

"Oh...grow up...grow up and comprehend." I thought my ears going nuts, Hearing to incredulous stuff.

"What...what did you say now?" George asked her instantly, when I got my sense.

"You can speak... r... how?" I asked her and wished she denies it. She admitted by keeping mum. I could not believe she can pronounce 'R' or again it was my illusion. "I don't believe this. Today I think it's my illusion and I wish..."

"No it isn't your illusion. It's only me..." Nobody from my companions was in a state to speak, yet my instincts provoked me.

"And what?" I was outrageous.

"Come on get up you silly, I want that thing give it to me." Merletta yelled. I was still under disbelief when suddenly George and both the Ma'am spring up from their place to fall into the Hellhole and I bellowed 'RAKSHA KAVACHAM' at once. This instant spell holds my companions back at their place and the transparent case spread around them.

"Oh… so you recalled everything." Merletta said loathingly.

"Merletta Why? What I have done to you?"

"Nothing you can do… but I can… anything for that thing." She said pointing towards the petal I held.

"Just because this you betrayed me, Merletta why? No, you can't do this. This is all Veronica's trick, she has definitely hexed you." "I told you so George, she played her turn. She has harmed everyone connected to me. Ma'am Merletta needs our help she is innocent she needs us… I'll …I'll surely get Veronica this time, Ma'am please help me"

"Herbriella don't go wild, calm down." Mrs. Brook shouldered me.

"Herbriella I want that just now." Merletta said stone heartedly. "This is mine."

"Obey me, you don't need this." The perfect order was given.

"What do you mean? Who are you?" she just smiled.

"Merletta don't you ever count her friendship? The days you have enjoyed together and the care she has always felt for you." Mrs. Brook said as if a Mum not able to see her own child's pain.

"You are not Merletta. I know you are Veronica … yes definitely you are the same old my enemy."

She just jerked her shoulders and mumbled. With the tremendous thunders the scope became murky and came down the two hanging human figure wrapped and tied with the thorny twigs swaying in the air. The bodies swayed right above the chasm.

"Merletta, we never expected from you." Mrs. Brook said, "I regret for letting you everything that you never had deserved."

"Herbriella is right, you are not the same, not at all worthy to her." Dr. Teasel taunted her sharply. "Who are you?"

She did not say anything and mumble on which the human bodies tied upward moved.

"A last chance for you to save them. Give me that and I will leave them."

"No, Herbriella do not listen to her. That's your last hope." Said George and the rest two agreed with him. I did not knew who were those humans but they were ought to be saved, anyhow.

"Okay, your wish." She again moved her lips and the chasm turned into hellhole. The fire burst out and reached near the victims. They bawled due to extreme heat. I was horribly shocked and felt giddy and was about to fell down when George held me. First thing I know them, Oh no! I looked towards George and even he got me.

How can I forget my chums? Mouzami and Nanisha were Veronica's prey and the cause for their situation was none other than Merletta- my favorite little girl. OH Mum I beg your help, I want to end all this, my heart screamed. I was in a deadly dilemma.

"I told you so; do not use your brains." Merletta looked more dangerous than our replicas right now.

"Merletta! You can't do this to my chums; I will not allow you... ever." Saying this I tried the spell on them that was effective for George, but nothing happened. Instead, my chums started going down gradually.

"Herbriea, don't panic, calm down and concentrate." Dr. Teasel said.

"Hurry! You are losing." Merletta tried her best.

"Herbriea, split the word IMPOSSIBLE." Mrs. Brook's roar encouraged me.

"Good Ma'am, but what about the word not applicable in my world." Said Merletta and chortled hellishly.

"Merletta, you want this petal, okay..."

"No, Herbriea, don't listen to her, don't you get in her scam."

"George, my chums. I cannot live on their cost." I was confused when I found myself unable to help my chums and hurt to see an innocent girl turning into evil. This trauma led me to burst into tears. I went on crying hiding my face with my palm; George and Dr. Teasel were consoling me when suddenly I felt the movement inside my fist that held the petal parts. The estranged parts moved with the help of my teardrops and joined to form an intact petal. So, this was the needful- my tears. Whatever, I was encouraged to move on. All the rest six eyes asked me not to give up. However, the question was how to stop my chums from going inside the Hellhole. If Merletta comes to know the petal, then what the guarantee she will leave my chum is, she lost my trust. Guruji had advised me not to rely on anyone though the dear ones and yes Merletta was the dearest one.

"George, I have to go there." I told them pointing towards Merletta.

"No you cannot." They all together denied.

"Don't want to say last good-bye to your chums, Herbriella?" said Merletta drawing us towards the Hellhole. I was forced to work on and I convinced all my friends this side. So I have to cross this Hellhole, but how.

"Don't even think to come here Herbriea; it's not your world." She got me and worried me. I closed my eyes and prayed for help. I opened my eyes and saw the climbers swaying above and…"SAHAYAM AHAM PRATI TARTI NARAKHA CHHIDRAM." I bellowed these words with my eyes shut. The climbers leaned down to form the bridge to cover the hellhole. I went on the bridge with an alarm and that rang. Merletta gave moment to her hands this time and crack down the bridge with force and I skipped a beat. The scope filled with tremendous screams as I decline along with the cracked bridge. Nevertheless, how can those teeny-weeny eyes bear this and obviously; the next moment I was beside Merletta with the help of climbers that clutched me.

"Poor Herbriella, now I can have you all at once." she covered herself inside the transparent thick trunk and laughed dangerously. I wonder why she is scared of me, when she is the one to be feared.

"Now you are out of your armor. You made it easy."

"How can you be so rude, Merletta?"

"Oh I love it, my job." She again laughed.

"Who are you?"

"I am the one to help people find their destiny, whoever comes in my way." She said with the utter carelessness. She looked concern towards the hellhole.

"So you killed Akka..." I got the meaning of her word 'help' and directly came to the point.

"Good...getting smart, start from the beginning, Christina- she was the first to fall into my way at the time of your birth. I smashed her beneath the concrete wall." Oh! No she chased me till now.

"I felt, I knew, I...told you so Herbriea... Christina was not killed in earthquake disaster... it was you to kill my sister... I will not leave you... you...," saying this George tried to reach us all a sudden, but Merletta raised her palm and threw the greenish smoke to bind him with the thorny twigs top to bottom but he could not remain bound too long as soon as he chanted the mantra 'JAI HANUMANJI MAHAVEER'

"Nevertheless Liz, I followed her and tried to grab her but she always was saved." She continued brutally.

"You witch; it was you to make my daughter inert, you heartless." Mrs. Brook kicked up a storm. I saw her this way for the first time.

"Kesar saw me on school terrace and she lost her life, even Gopi had to pay me." She again opened her black pages.

"Wha...at about Aa...kka's neighbor?" stammered Dr. Teasel.

I tried to grab their oblivious and moved towards Merletta.

"She heard me and saw me slaughtering Akka which I came to know while we were traveling by train, and I had to shut her mouth forever." She said viciously.

"Merletta, you will pay for this." Mrs. Brook cursed her.

Meantime, I looked for the way to seize her.

"Herbriella, it could be the biggest mistake of your life." Merletta stepped back as I moved ahead. She did not wait and spelled on the Hellhole, which turned into the deadly snaky hole full of snakes and her trunky armor too slithered towards me; yes I was trapped from all the sides. She was right it was my mistake. I had underestimated her. The slithers glided towards me cooling down my veins.

"Herbs use your spells." George shouted.

"Ha...Ha... a true bond, whatever I warned you." Merletta deride me. The glides speed up to entangle my legs and I went on moving to purge from them. Now it became must to get back along with my chums and desperately looked for any of my saviors. "SHAKHA AAGACHHATI ADHA CHA SAHAYAM AHAM" suddenly the words echoed. This worked out and the branches stretched in tearing out the ceiling pulled me upward. Within next seconds, I twine on the branches and pushed myself towards my chums, seized them and swiftly thrust them within the armor along with me. I dropped them safely among others, but the coil caught me. One snake drags me to plunge into the Hellhole. I struggled hard to get off and again tried spells in Sanskrit, but the hold went on stronger this time. Gradually it formed into the Monster- a snaky Monster.

"Careful!" Mrs. Brook, Dr.Teasel and George all together tried their best to pull me up. Merletta did not agree with them and mumbled again.

The second moment, all my saviors bounced in the air and flung far away. Mouzami and Nanisha were all right but perplexed. A monster was difficult to brawl. It dragged me inside the Hellhole almost and did not allow me to try even.

"Then how is this safe place?"

"But she is out of the safe place, Nani." I heard my chums arguing.

It was the moment when nasty creature heaved me, entirely and suddenly the glassy windows broke and the quaking of birds found the way towards me. Without wasting any time, the two peacocks smashed the ogre and released me smartly, yet I hanged on the edge. I climbed up with my chum's help and saw the lethal beaks shattering their prey randomly. Along with the huge one, they went on taking up others too. The deadly quacking and the hissings scratch out the ears.

[The movement of birds inside supported the movement outside too. The vicious creatures were smashed by the giant roots and the left over were taken up by the birds and butterflies.]

"I think only two cannot have the grand feast." George commented.

"But they are enough to swallow all." Mouzami said frantically.

"Look out." I said when Merletta flew above the Hellhole and came in our space forming another transparent barrier around her. All of us moved backward and I rushed towards the midst from where the flower rod had cropped up.

"So you won't give me that?" she asked me heading nearer to me.

"No way. After your soldier being smashed, I hope you don't desire to have the same." I held the rod and tried to find the way.

Suddenly, she cut herself half with her hand and there stood our replicas- another Herbriella and George. "So you were the one to run us down." I moved back as she headed, "You could have killed me before; you had many chances."

"I like to enjoy the every bit of my cuisine." She said carelessly.

"Then why you played our replicas, I was sure to come to get this without any exertions."

"No Pain, No Gain. How could you have your powers without being hurt? Moreover, I always help the people like you. Won't you count this my kindness?" each word of her wounded me.

"Just playing silly tricks you can't fear me."

"Oh really, then have the huge one now." Saying this she lifted her pinafore upward that turned into that same stinking blanket which was torn, as well. I felt some moment in my pocket and the torn part of the blanket flew away towards Merletta at once tearing away my dress. It obviously belonged to her.

"Ewe it's stinking, I can't bear it." Nanisha said. Merletta again turned around to take off her swelter robe and raised out the numerous snakes all over her body, even on her head and eyes and even the tongue. "Oh these are called Gorgons." Dr. Teasel said. This sudden and tremendous change shudder all us. The peacocks came back on their work, my buddies too tried to get closer, but all were instantly knock out by the fireball that Merletta has cast. They were petrified at the place; seemed she succeeded a step ahead. This really was huge. My hold tightened the rod and I tried to get the way. She consistently moved forward. I recalled all the spells in all the languages I knew, some of them were from Harry Potter, but nothing worked. Merletta…the Gorgon was proceeding towards me and I was there to watch her without any essence. My companions were yet unconscious leaving me to battle alone. The time was not to curse my brain to lurch at the end, as usual, but I was helpless. Lastly, I held the tail of positive, tried to drag it fully towards me and resolved to find out the way, anyhow.

Suddenly my eyes fell on the petal from which I got the last scalene stone, I saw the abrasion alike the sun in it and remembered the petal that joined with my tears had the similar mark of sun, so… I thought…I did… I squash the petal on to its place, and it burst out the flames that entered inside me and I was force down. With this, DHAM! DHAM! The entire scope was heard to be exploded.

Pin drop silence followed this extreme exertion. I was lying on the steps near the flower, totally burning mentally. I felt hot fire inside me top to bottom. Nobody from my friends was found nearby. I was now out of my mind. Only the one had the courage to slide up again towards me with its scattered parts.

"Herbriella, you are going to die now, get ready." Merletta, yet unable to join her crushed snaky parts, intently made the deadly move towards me and I tried to move but could not, felt I was jammed at the place. I watched the creepy things coiling and reaching my knees, yet I couldn't help out. I remembered my Mum's wish to find me my desired gift, well this I didn't mean. I saw my Mum's hopeless, worried face, yet I was helpless. Nor could I trust my fate and hope for anyone to pull me out from the darkness. I dropped the idea of getting released and got ready to be the biggest gift for Merletta. Though I tried to be calm, I wasn't, I was like burning internally. When Merletta's almost wrecked head at the rest of its strewn snaky twigs slithered towards me, suddenly my instincts grew, the current blazed me and I yelled at once "BHASMIBHUT NASHYATI" and amazing, instead of my words, the fire rays that emerged from my mouth blew her up. I got crazy and went on blowing until she and her left out scraps turned fully into ashes and slipped into the Hellhole winding the earth forever. As usual, I felt giddy and…

An Assignment

The fresh smell of fresh flowers along with fresh daylight filled in my nerves and I woke up. I checked my mouth and tongue; everything was perfect not even a hint of any heat passed through it. The petal of flower on which I had fixed all the parts of scalene stone got its color- it was RED. Rests of the Interiors were changed; there was no split flooring or any hodgepodge and not the sign of evils. Many unknown faces accompanied by my people filled the scope around me. The strangers were garbed royally and starring at me with smile. I did not wonder if they were from the other world.

"Your Highness, Congratulation! You got your powers." A woman in brilliant robes said. She was short and fair and looked on cloud nine.

"Thanks… but I am Herbriella and not any Highness or so and who are you?" but definitely it counts if I am the one amongst them.

"Sorry, you are very special and thus chosen for a very special deed." She replied hiding her identity.

"I have come here to finish my Mum's deed that she entrusted me, but I doubt I am anyway useful to you."

"It does not happen always, believe me you will reach your destination if you walk on the path just chosen for you."

"Can I have the person's name that has chosen the path for me?"

"Everything is hidden under his schedule and will be revealed at the relevant period." She said seeing upward and I got my Godmother. She sounds like Guruji.

"What if I don't get on my place?"

"You have already stepped towards."

"But she is very small to face such danger." Mrs. Brook expressed her worry for me.

"So what she has you people with her, always." She smiled proudly. "Moreover some others..." saying this she just lightly moved her hand clockwise and opened the outer surrounding of the Palace where the huge and tiny vegetation looked blissful greeting one another along with the various birds and butterflies as though they have won the battle and got their treasure right now. So this was the reason for my special sentiments with the nature, it was always with me and there came our ride Camel carrying us to the safest place, the tree that had transformed itself into the temporary shelter for us and Kalindi, putting the green bud into my pet kit. Then arrived Mr. Newman teaching me Sanskrit and everyone's eye fell on me. "Yes, he taught me Sanskrit." I said apologizing.

"Then he must be in danger." Mrs. Brook said.

"No need to worry, he is safe." The woman said and her weight increased for us. Therefore, all of them helped me without exposing themselves. Suddenly I remembered the teeny-weeny eyes...

"Whose eyes are that I see now and then?" I asked the woman from the other world.

"That is your foresight and that makes you different." She replied after a while.

"And why she needed that petal?"

"She didn't want you to have your powers."

"Who was she? Who am I?"

"You definitely will find out."

"Oh no, I don't want to live restless?"

"Are you sure?" And she gazed at me.

"Ok...What I have to do?"

"Well, you will be rewarded for that." She was talking about my firepower, I think.

"We will have to come here each time?" asked George.

"Can't say." She replied calmly.

"So I will have this deadly duel again?" I was eager.

"Well, maybe." She replied.

"But how will I know?

"I emphasize on your soul, your deeds are rebound to you as returns, whether good or bad." She was not annoyed.

"But to walk on the way means to have more loss in place of me." I said anxiously.

"Their sacrifice should not be cry over. Instead realize the ways the nature has helped you." She again moved her hand clockwise and with this the two savior Peacocks appeared and bowed in front of me. I was embarrassed to have the honor that I was supposed to give them to save my friends life and me. The beautiful woman clapped this time and smiled at me. The two proud birds turned into human figures with their head down.

"Congratulation, your Highness!" saying this they both raised their head keeping us in BIGGEST AWE.

"VERONICA! LIAL!" Including me, my mates on this earth quivered the entire scope.

"Yes Ma'am, George, Mouzami, Nanisha and … Your Highness; we were always present whenever you were in danger." I saw her smiling for the first time ever since.

"I thought you were the cause… sorry, but yet it is incredible."

"I know. It was my job to harass you to unearth your instincts." One by one, I recalled the brightest role they both have played saving me each time and thus they were present whenever Merletta linger around me. Really to figure out the Good and Evil is the huge deal.

"So it was you to smash, that snake near the Kalindi's tent." I asked Lial.

"Yes, I finished the one and failed to get the other. Owing to the law of nature, we did not accompany you at the mountain as well."

"Oh Jesus, I misunderstood you, always. But Veronica why did you steal Merletta's school badge and placed it in Mouzami's book?"

"Merletta herself did this to make you alone from your friends."

"She purposely sent you out of the room proving her missing. But I caught her as she had never guessed me as your savior. I had jinxed her at the same place, anyhow she rescued. Lial and I followed you in Palace and were able to serve you our best."

"Oh, how stupid of us to take you wrong, we are sorry Veronica." Mouzami said.

"It wasn't your fault. We were bound to make you aware." Veronica said. She then took out something from behind and gave it to me. It was my Mum's antique box that I thought to be lost. The bloomed flowers were shining inside.

"I am sorry for taking this without your consent."

"Herbriella, this will be your useful companion, if you wish."

"Your Highness, we are extremely sorry to misbehave with you." Lial said bending as if waiting to be punished.

"Don't call me that, I am your friend and you deserve this." I raised him and hugged both of them. George and my chums joined us too. Suddenly the wind stopped blowing, the noise around was not heard now, seemed the world has ceased breathing and the celestial brightness increased at its last as the heavenly bodies started haul up towards the sky with Veronica and Lial, too.

"No, you cannot go." I tried to pull them.

"We have to Your Highness… sorry Herbriea." They said and slowly moved upward. I approached that beautiful woman.

"You say I am the Princess than tell them to stay …"

"Sorry, their duty ceases for the time being. You will find them on the word of event."

"At least tell me who are you?"

"You can remember me as Erica." Saying this she followed her people in the air, leaving me down to solve bunches of mysteries.

"HERBRIELLA, HELP!" Nanisha's scream gets me back on the earth. The branches trapped her and my other pals were ready to follow her when I said, "PRAKRUTI SAHAYAM AHAM." We were thrown on the hot sand, but the exteriors were different, hottest than the sand. The battle of Pharaohs fighting ahead made us hurdle.

"Oh! No! What is this place? Where we have come?" asked Dr. Teasel getting up hardly out of the sand. Mrs. Brook was mopping out the sand that had stuck to their elbows and knees. Mouzami was trying to drag Nanisha out of the dale of sand. George was smiling beside me and suddenly, a tiger's descendant mewed falling into my lap and I said, "In the field of 'CATS'.

The End